06/24
STAND PRICE
$ 5.00

when pirates
came to brooklyn

OTHER BOOKS BY
Phyllis Shalant

Bartleby of the Mighty Mississippi

The Great Eye

Beware of Kissing Lizard Lips

Shalom, Geneva Peace

The Transformation of Faith Futterman

The Rock Star, the Rooster, and Me, the Reporter

when pirates came to Brooklyn

Phyllis Shalant

Dutton Children's Books • *New York*

This book is a work of fiction. Names, characters, places, and incidents are either the product of the author's imagination or are used fictitiously, and any resemblance to actual persons, living or dead, business establishments, events, or locales is entirely coincidental.

Copyright © 2002 by Phyllis Shalant

All rights reserved. No part of this publication may be reproduced or transmitted in any form or by any means, electronic or mechanical, including photocopying, recording, or any information storage and retrieval system now known or to be invented, without permission in writing from the publisher, except by a reviewer who wishes to quote brief passages in connection with a review written for inclusion in a magazine, newspaper, or broadcast.

CIP Data is available.

Published in the United States by Dutton Children's Books,
a division of Penguin Putnam Books for Young Readers
345 Hudson Street, New York, New York 10014
www.penguinputnam.com
Designed by Richard Amari
Printed in USA   First Edition
1 3 5 7 9 10 8 6 4 2
ISBN 0-525-46920-6

To Joseph Shalant and Frances Shalant and, always,
for the ones who know my heart—Donnabee and Herb

Special thanks to Mrs. Stephanie Badulak
and the students at Stackpole Elementary School

when pirates
came to brooklyn

1

I was walking along Avenue J, kicking a silvery pebble down the sidewalk, when the roses called to me. "Hey, girl! Do you believe in enchanted flowers?"

I stopped and stared over the green iron fence. "No, I do not."

The roses giggled. "Then why are you talking to us?" They were ruby red, like the kind in fairy tales, and they were climbing and twisting all over a trellis that hid the backyard from passersby like me.

I gazed at the big white house beside the trellis. A covered porch was wrapped around its side, snug as a best friend's arm around your waist. Beneath the roof, two half-moon attic windows seemed to be winking at me.

"Because I thought it was this old maple speaking," I answered, nodding at a branch overhead. "Trees are big talkers."

"They are?" This time the roses spoke in a high, squeaky voice. For a moment, I thought I saw something coppery move behind them.

"Yes, but they don't talk to everyone. Trees are very particular." I patted the gray-brown trunk like it was an old friend, and leaned against it. I could feel the roses watching while I pulled up my kneesocks and retied my shoes.

"Well, good-bye," I announced when I was through. "Maybe I'll see you again tomorrow." Then I ran off before they could say another word.

2

Of course, that big white house didn't just pop up like toast from a toaster. I'd always known it was there on the corner of Avenue J and East Thirty-eighth Street, right on my route home from school. You couldn't miss it because it was so unlike the other houses in our neighborhood, which were as plain and crumbly as slices of stale white bread.

But before sixth grade, I always ran straight home from school. I'd sprint up the stairs to our fourth-floor apartment without stopping once on the landings. Then, after I dropped off my books, kissed my mother, and tickled the baby, I'd run back down to the third floor—because that was where my best friend, Deb Greenberg, was waiting for me.

I couldn't really remember Deb before she needed a wheelchair. She was six when she got polio, but I'd only been four then. It just seemed natural to me that Deb's mother and father carried her downstairs every morning to wait for the van that took her away to a special school.

When she returned, our super, Zeke Mayfield, helped Mrs. Greenberg carry Deb back up again. She usually spent the rest of the afternoon indoors. Deb's long legs were as thin as Popsicle sticks, but lugging her and the chair up and down was awfully hard on her mother.

It didn't seem fair that there wasn't an elevator for the people in our building, especially since there was one for our garbage. Even though it was 1960, we still used a stinky old dumbwaiter instead of an incinerator like the one in the more modern apartment house across the street. Every night at eight o'clock, Zeke would ring a bell that was the signal for me to take the greasy brown bag from the kitchen to the little square door in our foyer. Then I'd open it and wait for the wooden dumbwaiter box that stopped on each floor, just like an elevator.

After I shoved our bag into the box, I'd shout, "Okay, Zeke," down the dark, drafty shaft. And from the basement, he'd pull on the ropes that sent the creaky thing down to the garbage room again.

There were thirty-six apartments to collect trash from each day. Sometimes I wondered if Zeke minded his job. He was more polite than any adult I knew—even to us kids. But I noticed that around grown-ups, he didn't smile as much or say more than he needed to.

I never really cared about having to play indoors with Deb. Her room was full of things to do, like board games and arts and crafts. Best of all was her two-story dollhouse, which was made of wood and had a fireplace, rugs, and electric lights.

We spent almost every day playing with that house and its miniature plastic family, whom we called "the Weenies." Deb was always Mrs. Weenie and the girl doll, Teena Weenie. I was Mr. Weenie and the boy doll, Jimmy Weenie. Sometimes we'd pretend Teena was having a party with movie actors and actresses (played by cutouts from Deb's stack of movie-star magazines). Or we drew faces on Mrs. Greenberg's wooden clothespins to create robbers who climbed in through the windows while the dollhouse family slept. (Teena and Jimmy always captured them.) Or the family adopted an amazing new pet like a donkey, an elephant, or a swan from Deb's collection of glass animals.

Every night before I fell asleep, I thought up new adventures for the Weenies. I could hardly wait till the next afternoon to try them out. But the summer before sixth grade (Deb was going into seventh), Mrs.

Greenberg mentioned to my mom that Deb was getting too heavy to be carried up and down in the wheelchair. Then, at the end of August, right before school began, the Greenbergs bought a house—in faraway Briny Breezes, Florida.

"We chose a ranch house so there wouldn't be any stairs to climb," I heard Mrs. Greenberg tell my mother. "Deborah will finally be able to get out and play with girls her own age."

I'd never thought Deb cared how old I was. I'd never minded that she was a little bossy.

The night before they moved out, Mr. Greenberg carried the dollhouse upstairs to our apartment. "Deb wants you to have this, Lee," he said. "She says she's too old for it."

I stepped back while he struggled to bring the bulky dollhouse inside. I was concentrating so hard on swallowing back tears, I'm not even sure I said thank you.

3

At two-thirty, I was supposed to be writing about the latest photo from Miss Hadley's collection of *Life* magazines. Each week, she tacked up a different picture and let us write whatever we wanted. "Create a story, a poem, a description, or just tell about what the picture makes you feel," she'd said. "Just as long as you're *writing*."

Usually, I liked writing time. But today I couldn't stop thinking about the talking roses. I was planning to see them the minute school was out. When Miss Hadley wasn't watching, I slid two marble-covered notebooks, my thick blue reader, and a math book onto my knees. Then I put my pencil case on top, trying to keep it from rattling. The hardest part was fastening my red rubber bookstrap without letting it snap.

Across the aisle from me, Eddie Wagner was using the metal tip of a compass to dig into the soft, stained wood of his desktop. When he saw what I was doing, he smirked like we were conspirators in crime. I turned away quickly, but he'd already caught me looking at him. *Ick!* I didn't want Eddie thinking I was anything like him. His desktop was covered with disgusting drawings, like a gun shooting at a rat and the top half of a naked woman. He hardly ever did his homework, he never raised his hand, and if the teacher called on him, his only answer was a shrug. Eddie was new at our school this year. Everyone said he'd come because his old school had thrown him out. I don't think anyone had actually asked him about it, but it seemed like it could be true.

To keep my eyes from sliding toward Eddie again, I stared hard at the photo. This time it was a funny one—a bulldog with a parrot sitting on its head. Luckily, an idea came to me:

Bob the bulldog was pleased whenever Paco the parrot sat on his head. When people spoke to Bob, they only said, "Sit!" or "Stay!" or "Roll Over!" But Paco asked Bob interesting questions, like how it felt to be covered in fur and what dogs dreamed about. Bob thought . . .

Brriiing! At the sound of the three o'clock bell, I jumped up without finishing my sentence. Before anyone else even got to the coat closet, I snatched my red sweater off its hook and raced to the door. Just as I was leaving, something made me look back at Eddie. He was still smirking at me. *Double-ick!*

This time, instead of talking roses, I found three heads poking over the porch rail of the big white house. They looked as if they were waiting for someone.

One of them belonged to a girl with braids the color of lemon drops. She bobbed high over the other two as she called out, "Hey! Would you like to come up here?" She reminded me of a scarecrow with her wide smile and blurry blue eyes that looked painted on behind pink eyeglasses. The other kids, a boy and a girl, were both coppery redheads. They waved to me as if we'd already met.

"Okay, I guess." I followed the fence around to the porch steps, careful not to run so they wouldn't know how excited I was.

The scarecrow girl did all the talking. "I'm Polly Burke. This is Eileen Kilkenny and her brother, Timmy. What's your name?" I liked her short, cute nose and the way her smile seemed to take up half her face.

"Lee Bloom," I answered, speaking extra clearly because being up on the porch was like being on a stage. I could see other kids walking home from school, and I knew they saw me, too.

"We're having a shipwreck. We need another person to help us," Polly explained, even though there wasn't an ocean, a river, or a puddle in sight. "Come on, let's go inside."

"Inside?" I repeated dumbly.

"That's where the shipwreck is. You'll see."

Part of me wanted to stay on the porch, watching people and traffic pass, as if I were a princess overseeing her kingdom. Another part was itching to find out what kind of shipwreck could be indoors. But there was a third part, too—a little voice saying I wasn't supposed to enter strangers' houses, even if this stranger was just a tall, skinny girl. That voice sounded just like my mother's.

Polly opened the door and slipped inside with the coppery heads right behind. I stayed on the porch, unsure what to do, until I thought of the For Rent sign outside our building and Deb's empty apartment.

"Lee, are you coming?" Polly's head peeked out of the door again.

"Yes!" I grabbed my books and hurried inside.

"Just leave those in the vestibule," she called as she dashed up a staircase.

I'd never heard the word *vestibule* before, but I could tell it meant the little entrance room before you stepped into the main part of the house. Polly's had a bench with a hinged seat that opened like a lid. It looked like a place to store treasure, like strings of pearls and gold coins. I lifted the lid for a second to peek, but there was only a jumble of boots and old toys—rusty ice skates, a bald doll, and a volleyball that needed air. I shut the bench top and set my books and sweater on it.

"We're going up to the attic!" Polly shouted from above.

I started up the stairs after the others. The house smelled different from mine. It reminded me of overripe fruit and stale air, as if the windows didn't get opened much. My house smelled mostly of my mother's cooking. On the way to school some mornings, I could still smell roast chicken or brisket in my hair.

On the second floor, a line of dark doors stood shut up and gloomy. As quickly as possible, I dashed up the next staircase. It was much steeper and narrower than the first. Each stair squeaked sharply as if it were insulted that I'd stepped on it.

At the top of the landing, Polly was waiting in

front of a bright green door. "You've got to pass Sir Beetlebug to get inside," she said. She nodded at a knight who appeared to be guarding the entrance. He was dressed in armor right down to his mesh gloves. His left hand held a spear. Yet the top of his helmet only came up to my chin.

"He's so small!" For some reason I was whispering.

"We think he was only a boy," Polly replied. "They probably locked him into this suit when he was just six or seven. That's how they did it in the olden days."

"Who did it?"

"The head knight and his men." Polly seemed so serious, I wasn't sure if she was making it up. "They locked up little boys like Timmy in these suits until they got old enough to fight. You only had to be eleven or twelve to be in the king's service."

"Really?" I touched Sir Beetlebug's arm with one finger. "If he was locked in, how did he grow?"

"Probably his bones just got all bent up and twisty. I bet the pain made him really ferocious. Sometimes at night, it sounds like his spirit's moaning up here. Poor old Beetlebug." Polly tapped him on the helmet. The hollow sound of empty armor echoed sadly.

"Aaahhh! HELP! SAVE ME!"

"POLLY! LEE! HURRY!"

I felt my flesh turning to metal.

"Come on!" Polly's hand locked around my wrist. In an instant, she jerked me past Sir Beetlebug and through the green door.

4

The attic was a big empty box of a place. Its floor was smooth, bare wood, and there was hardly any furniture at all—just two dark blue couches that faced each other across the sunny room. Eileen and Timmy were jumping up and down on one of them.

"S-O-S! S-O-S! The ship's going down!" Eileen bellowed. "Man the lifeboat, Tim!"

"Aye, aye, sir." Timmy threw one of the couch cushions onto the floor. Then he jumped on it and sat, rocking back and forth as Eileen got on behind him. Together they began propelling their raft with their arms.

Polly swept another cushion onto the floor and turned to me. "We'll be the pirates. I'm captain and you're first mate. Let's capture them!" She knelt on the cushion and motioned for me to get behind her.

My heart thumped like one of the decrepit washers in our basement as I jumped on board. Polly and I pushed with our arms and legs, and our pirate galleon slid across the shiny floor.

"We'd better destroy their raft," Polly yelled.

Eileen and Timmy tried to paddle away, but we surged forward and crashed into them. Whooping and screaming, they rolled onto the floor.

"Help me, I'm drowning!" Eileen stretched out a freckled arm.

"Me, too!" Timmy flailed his arms, coughing as though he'd swallowed too much salty water.

"What should we do?" Polly asked me.

I looked over at Eileen and Timmy. "We could pull them aboard and make them be pirates, too . . . or we could just steal their raft."

"Oh no—sharks! Sharks are coming!" Eileen shrieked even louder. She was the best screamer I'd ever heard. I could barely scream at all, not even in the schoolyard at recess. It was probably due to lack of practice. According to my mother, living in an apartment meant no screaming unless you were dying. *Really dying.* Otherwise the neighbors would complain and your whole family could be evicted.

"Here sharky, sharky," Polly sang. "Come get your dinner. Yummy Eileen stew and tasty Timmy pudding." She stuck out her tongue and licked her upper lip.

"No! No!" Eileen wailed.

"Keep away, you sharks you." Timmy's hands were balled in fists, and his face was all pinched up. He sounded fierce, but he looked like he was trying not to cry.

"Maybe we should save them," I said. "They can cook the meals and scrub the deck. Later, if we're bored, we can make them walk the plank."

"Oh, all right." Polly reached over for another cushion and lined it up behind ours. "Here, you two ride in the dinghy."

"Thank you, thank you!" Eileen dragged herself and Timmy onto the new boat. But as soon as she was settled, she pointed a freckled finger at something. "Look! Look! THERE'S A TYPHOON COMING. What should we do?"

I glanced over my shoulder. A big, purple cloud was rising up from the waves. It whirled toward us, rushing and roaring. It looked exactly like the typhoon I'd seen on a TV commercial for floor cleaner—a smiling woman opened a bottle and a great cloud swirled out over her kitchen linoleum, leaving it sparkling. Then she whistled and the cloud whooshed back into the bottle.

"We're doomed, we're doomed," Eileen moaned.

"Maybe we could trap it in a bottle," I suggested.

"Yes, a bottle would be great," Polly agreed. "Then we could take it to school and let it out in class."

A huge smile spread over Timmy's face. He glanced at his sister. "Just like a giant stinkeroo!"

"Timmy!" Eileen pushed him overboard.

We all started giggling. Eileen's high-pitched laugh sounded like a crazy bird's. Strands of hair the color of new pennies had escaped from her white plastic headband and were hanging in front of her round face. She flopped onto her back and waved her arms and legs in the air. I'd never met anyone who laughed or screamed from head to toe the way she did.

We rolled off the cushions onto the floor. I laughed so much, my sides began hurting and I had to hug myself. Finally, Timmy sat up on his knees. "What school do you go to, Lee?"

"P.S. 119." The P.S. stood for "Public School," but I'd never heard anyone use anything but the initials.

"Is that the one on the next block?"

I nodded.

"Eileen and I go to Holy Rosary. I'm in second grade and she's in fifth."

"I'm in sixth." I didn't mention that I'd be in fifth grade like Eileen if I hadn't skipped fourth grade the year before last. A lot of kids didn't like skippers. The younger ones thought we were know-it-alls, and the older ones thought we were babies. Either way, we got ignored or teased.

"Are you Catholic?"

"Nope." I sat up and smoothed out the pleats of my gray skirt. Suddenly we were all quiet, like we'd used up our supply of shouting and laughing for the day.

"What are you?" Timmy asked.

Underneath her freckles, Eileen's wide cheeks got all pink. "Quit asking so many questions, Tim!"

"I don't care," I said, but a finger of something flicked at my throat. "I'm Jewish."

Timmy's eyes were round and unblinking. "Robby Donovan says the Jews killed Jesus."

"Timmy!" Eileen smacked him on the back of his neck. "Sorry," she told me, wincing as if what Timmy had said was her fault.

"It's okay." Suddenly I sounded as if I had a sore throat. I'd heard those things said against Jews before. At recess last year, I'd been playing jacks in the school-yard with Mary Ellen Munson, when some older girls I didn't recognize came and stood outside the fence. *"Hey Jew-girls!"* they'd shouted at us. *"You killed Jesus. We're gonna get you!"*

Mary Ellen was not even Jewish, but we'd grabbed hands and dashed into the building. We didn't stop running until we reached the fountain outside our classroom, where we drank and drank as if what those girls yelled had dried us out. But Mary Ellen and I didn't say a word to each other about what had happened—ever.

"I wish I went to school around here. I hate mine," Polly said.

"Where do you go?" I asked.

"Divine Revelations Academy." Polly sounded like she'd caught my sore throat. "It's for the kids that attend our church. I'm in sixth grade, but the school's so small, we have fourth, fifth, and sixth in one room."

That didn't seem so bad to me. If we'd had three grades together at P.S. 119, no one would've noticed who'd skipped.

"I hate school, too," Eileen said. "This year I have Sister Margaret Rose. When she gets mad at you, she whacks your hand with a ruler."

"Brother John whacked Robby Donovan for saying 'Jeezus Beezus' when he got thrown out at home plate during recess," Timmy announced.

I couldn't imagine Miss Hadley hitting anyone. I didn't think it was allowed at our school. Miss Hadley never even used the words *mad* or *angry*. She only said, "Boys and girls, I'm getting really peeved at you."

Downstairs, a door slammed. "Polly?" a voice called.

"My mom's home from work." Polly stood up and brushed off her skirt.

Eileen jumped up. "Oh, Timmy, we're late! I was supposed to heat up the stew. Mother's going to be steamed as a baked potato at me."

I imagined her mother, a red-haired Mrs. Potato Head, with steam coming out of her ears. I never had to do anything in the kitchen except set the table.

When I looked out the window, I was surprised to see how low the sun was. Three blocks away, I could make out the top of my apartment building. A sudden pang of hunger told me it was almost dinnertime.

"I'd better go, too," I said.

Before anyone moved, the attic door groaned open. Quickly, Polly smoothed her hair. "Hi, Mom."

"Hello, Mrs. Burke," Eileen said, tucking her creased white blouse into her waistband. Timmy seemed to shrink into her side.

I tried to smile, but it wasn't easy because Polly's mother was staring at me. Her hair was the dull color of sparrow feathers, and her eyes were small and dark like a bird's under her thin, arched eyebrows. Her bony hand clutched at Polly's shoulder.

"This is Lee Bloom," Polly said.

The birdy eyes landed on me. "Do you live on Avenue J, Lee?"

"Yes."

"I believe I know your parents. Your father purchased a small policy from Mr. Burke when you were born."

"Oh," I murmured. I didn't even know what a policy was.

Mrs. Burke smiled with her mouth closed.

"We have to go home now." Eileen tugged Timmy by the arm. The two of them began backing toward the attic door.

I picked up a cushion and set it on the sofa. Mrs. Burke's stare was making me twitchy. I actually jumped when Polly plucked at my sleeve.

"Do you want to come over tomorrow?" Polly's eyes were so fixed on mine, it was as if her mother wasn't even there.

"Okay—I'll see if I can." I said it kind of quietly because her mother was watching. But inside my chest, my heart was doing the lindy hop.

I held my breath as I slipped past Sir Beetlebug and

bounded down to the vestibule. I was nearly out the front door when I realized I'd forgotten something. "Thank you!" I called out—but no one answered. The house seemed as silent as if it were empty. Or as if it had fallen under a spell.

5

Instead of going straight home, I headed for one of my hiding places—the one at the base of a giant oak around the block from my apartment building. It was a space between the roots most people wouldn't notice—only three fingers wide, but deep and dark. On the way to school that morning, I'd hidden a nickel inside it as a test. If the coin was there on the way home, I'd know the place was still secret. If not, I'd have to do without the candy bar I'd been saving it for.

I looked up and down the block to be sure no one was watching. Then I crouched down and felt between the roots. But all I touched was wood, soft dirt, and something crawly. I tried to peer into the crevice.

"Did you lose something?"

I looked back over my shoulder and saw Eddie Wagner. Where had he come from so fast? "Uh—no.

I mean, I might have dropped something in there." I stood up and faced him.

Eddie tossed his scraggly hair out of his eyes with a jerk of his head. Grinning, he reached into the pocket of his thin, blue jacket, pulled out a Snickers bar, and began unwrapping it.

A cry of anger rose up in my throat, but I forced it back down. Maybe Eddie had taken my nickel, but I had no proof. My uncle Harold, who was a lawyer, once told me never to accuse anyone unless I had evidence to back me up.

I picked the dirt from under my nails. "What are you doing here?"

Eddie shrugged and took a big bite of candy.

I was pretty sure he'd moved nearby. I'd spotted him on the street, around the houses with the cracked driveways. And once I even saw him in the alley behind my building. But I always acted like I didn't notice him. He'd never acted like he'd seen me, either.

"Want some?" Eddie held the gooey chocolate toward me. It had fingerprints and tooth marks on it. I didn't think I could ever eat another Snickers.

"No, thank you. I've got to get home." I scooped my books off the sidewalk.

"What for?" Eddie smacked his lips and took another bite of candy. One of his front teeth was chipped and pointy like a dog's. "To do your homework, *Skippy?*"

"Who told you I skipped?" I could already feel my face turning red. Eddie was such a jerk. I should've ignored him, but it was too late. Now he knew how to make me mad.

"Too bad you can't go back to your old school," I said to his sneering face. "What did you do—steal someone's lunch money?"

"Yeah," Eddie said, although I wasn't really expecting an answer. He threw the rest of the Snickers on the ground and walked away. I guess I knew how to make him mad, too.

But I had more important things to think about on the way home—my hiding places. Now I only had two. One was along the row of boxwoods that made a hedge around my apartment building. I could actually fit my whole self into that one. The other was inside the electrical box on the traffic light opposite school. One day while I was waiting to cross, I'd noticed that I could pry open the little door on the box and fit something small in between the wires.

Even though I didn't use them much, it felt important to have those hiding places. Our apartment wasn't anything like the Burkes' big house. I had to share a room with the baby, and my parents had to sleep on a convertible sofa in the living room. Our place was too small to keep anything secret.

In the lobby of our building, Zeke was washing the floors and whistling loudly to himself. I tiptoed around the edges so I wouldn't leave footprints.

"Hello, Lee," he said when he saw me. "How is Deborah doing in Florida?" Except for Deb's mother, Zeke was the only person who ever called Deb "Deborah." His speech was more formal than most people's. He always said "did not" for "didn't," and "I am" for "I'm."

"I don't know. Deb hasn't written," I told him.

"Oh? Well, I suppose she is still getting settled. I am sure you will hear from her soon."

"I guess so."

Zeke pushed up the brim of the tan peaked cap he always wore. "I wanted to talk to you about something."

I wondered if one of the neighbors had complained about my running up and down the stairs. Some of the older people in the building were very grouchy about noise. I stared into his broad, brown face, which was always moving, just like the rest of him. "Okay, what?"

"I was cleaning out the bicycle and carriage room

this morning, and I found a bike that was left by some tenants who moved away a long time ago. It looks like the right size for you. I thought you might have some time to ride it."

I didn't especially like biking. I wasn't even sure I remembered how to ride. The last time I'd had a bike, I'd been five. My aunt and uncle had gotten me one while my mother was in the hospital. Every day, Aunt Bea would take me outside to ride it back and forth in front of our building. After a while, I'd insisted I didn't need training wheels anymore. I'd nagged until Aunt Bea had given in and asked Zeke to remove them. And for the next few days, Zeke held on to the back of the seat while I rode, because Aunt Bea got too out of breath when she ran.

Finally, when my aunt was convinced I wasn't going to fall, Zeke let go. After that, I rode back and forth without training wheels. But the whole time I was riding, I was really just waiting for Mom to reappear. When she finally did, I quit. I didn't even notice when I outgrew the little bike. It was still down in the basement, waiting for Mikey, my baby brother.

Now it looked like I could use a bike. If I had one, I'd ride all over Brooklyn, discovering secret places. I could have so many, I'd have to write them down in a notebook to keep track of them.

"I would like to have a bike," I told Zeke. "I just hope I still remember how to ride."

"Of course you will. Ask your mother if you may have it. If she says yes, you can see it tomorrow after school."

"Okay, Zeke. Thanks."

The heavenly smell of Bloom chicken soup flooded the hallway when Mom opened the door. "Lee, where were you today?" She was carrying Mikey in one arm. When she bent down to kiss me, he hit me on the head with a rubber teething ring.

"I was playing with some kids," I said, tickling Mikey's neck.

"You see? I knew once you stopped moping around about Deb you'd find plenty of friends at school."

I followed her into the kitchen without saying anything. Mom had funny ideas about being a kid. She thought just because you lived on the same block, or were in the same class as another boy or girl, you would be friends.

"So who are these new pals?" Mom handed me a carrot stick. She put Mikey into his high chair and gave him a soft, cooked one, droopy as a noodle.

"They're just kids."

My mother gave me a look.

"From the neighborhood."

"Where exactly in the neighborhood?" Mom asked, raising her voice a bit. She began pinching wilted blossoms off the violets she grew on the windowsill.

I took a bite of carrot and chewed it slowly. "You know that big white house on the corner of East Thirty-eighth?"

"Yes."

"One of them lives there. A girl."

"In that big place! What's her name?"

"Polly Burke."

My mother's face seemed to crack a bit.

"Her mother said she knows Daddy. She told me he bought a policy when I was born."

"The Burkes have an insurance agency," Mom said. All the interest had gone out of her voice. She went back to fussing with her plants. She didn't ask who else I'd met or anything more about my new friends.

I crunched down hard on my carrot again. "Zeke found an old bike in the storage room. He thinks it might be the right size for me."

"We can't afford a bike right now," my mother answered. "Maybe for your birthday."

"You wouldn't have to pay anything. It's one that somebody doesn't want anymore."

Mom just shook her head no.

"But Zeke *wants* to give it to me."

"It's inappropriate. A bicycle from a schwar—from the superintendent."

I knew she'd almost said *schwartzer* before she caught herself. It was a Yiddish word that meant "Negro." Mom was more careful around me now, but I could remember her saying it often when I was little, especially when we rode the bus downtown to go shopping. That was where a lot of Negroes lived and worked. But in our neighborhood there were hardly any that I knew of, except for the nurse's aide who came to help Mrs. Feldman in 4D, the man who raked leaves at the park, and Zeke and Mrs. Mayfield, of course. Even my school only had two Negro kids in it—and they were sister and brother.

I didn't see what Zeke's color had to do with my getting a bike. I glared at my mother.

"I don't want you taking anything from him." Mom turned her back to scrub the counter, though it was white as a new sheet of paper.

"You give the clothes I outgrow to Mrs. Mayfield," I argued. Zeke and his wife, Mary, didn't have any children of their own, but Mrs. Mayfield had nieces in Tennessee. "Why can't I have an outgrown bike? It would be like a trade."

"That's enough, Lee."

"You don't like anyone, but other—"

"Lee!" My mother's shoulders were raised up like the back of an angry cat.

I shut up then. Mom was easily upset on account of all the heartaches she'd had. Once, before Mikey was born, she'd become so sad, she'd had to stay in a hospital. That was when Aunt Bea had moved in to help Dad take care of me.

After dinner, I finally wrote a letter to Deb. I don't know why I hadn't done it yet. Maybe I was hoping she would send me one first.

> *Dear Deb,*
>
> *How are things in Florida? I guess you are busy with all the horses and cows at your ranch house (ha! ha!). Now that you can get outside more, you've probably made a lot of new friends. I guess you are doing junior high-type things with them. Are you taking French like you said you would?*
>
> *I met some new kids. One of them is named Polly, and she lives in an amazing house. Today we had a*

shipwreck inside. It was almost as if we were real live Weenies (ha! ha!).

The true Weenies told me to say they miss you a lot.

Love,

Lee

P.S. Write Back!

6

The next morning I gulped down my juice, ate my egg in four bites, and wrapped my toast in a napkin. "I have to be early today," I told Mom as I shoved the toast into one of the big, deep pockets of my sweater.

Actually, I had things to do *before* I got to school. I raced down Avenue J without stopping until I got to the Burkes' house. *Must do something VERY IMPORTANT right after school. Will try to come over later. —Lee Bloom,* I wrote on a piece of notebook paper. I folded it twice and tucked it into one of the swirls in the green iron fence before I hurried on.

My next stop was the electrical box on the traffic light opposite school. Unfortunately, a lot of kids were crossing there. I had to stand around pretending I was waiting for someone until the block was clear. Then I reached into the pocket of my sweater and pulled out Teena Weenie. Quickly, I pried open the door on the box, popped her inside, and shut the door again. "See you later," I whispered, and ran across the street just in time for the nine o'clock bell.

The first thing I noticed as I walked into the classroom was the blackboard. Miss Hadley had written BIOGRAPHY PROJECT TODAY in letters about a foot high. When I saw the row of tan-covered books along the windowsill, I couldn't help sighing. I didn't usually like reading books that weren't stories. But Miss Hadley was interested in everything—and she thought we should be, too.

The surfaces in our classroom were covered with stuff she'd bought, or found, or cut out of magazines and newspapers. On top of the bookcase was a bottle filled with layers of red, pink, green, and brown sand that she'd gotten in the Painted Desert. The paperweight on her desk—a cracked rock filled with purple crystals—was actually a geode from the Grand Canyon. Even the door to the coat closet was covered with one of her souvenirs—a picture of a pond full of soft-colored water lilies with a little curved bridge in the background. Miss Hadley told us she'd seen the real-life pond when she'd visited the painter's home in France.

When everyone was seated, Miss Hadley glided

over to the windowsill. "The men and women in these books were once boys and girls like yourselves. They had special interests and talents like you, and sometimes they were mischievous or just plain ornery like you." She held up one of the books. "The inventor Thomas Edison couldn't stop asking questions. Thomas's constant curiosity so irritated his teacher that he gave Thomas a whipping! But fortunately, Thomas's mother knew asking questions was a good thing. She took her son out of school and taught him herself."

Miss Hadley held up the book on Edison as if it were a prize. "Now, who thinks he or she might want to be a scientist?"

Several hands shot up.

"All right, Mitchell. This is for you. But don't let Mr. Edison give you any ideas about dropping out of school."

Across the aisle from me, Eddie snickered. We all knew Mitchell was Mr. Perfect. He never missed a day of school.

Miss Hadley chose another book and studied the spine. "Who might want to be a nurse?"

A lot of girls raised their hands. Not me. Mrs. Feldman, our neighbor in 4D, was always sick. Whenever Mom cooked chicken soup, she made me take her a container. The moldy medicine smell in her apartment made me nauseous, but I had to wait there while Mrs. Feldman found me a treat like a half-eaten roll of Life Savers or an ancient flowered hankie.

I didn't think I'd make a very good nurse or scientist. And although I loved Miss Hadley, I didn't think I'd be a good teacher, either. I just wasn't patient or calm like she was. I used to want to be a movie actress, until one day Uncle Harold heard me arguing with Mom.

"Lee, if you weren't a girl, you'd make a great lawyer," he'd told me.

"Aren't there any girl lawyers?" I'd asked.

"Not too many," Uncle Harold answered.

That made me want to be one.

Miss Hadley handed out *Benjamin Franklin*, *Louis Pasteur*, *Madame Curie*, *Betsy Ross*, and *George Washington*. There weren't any books about girl lawyers. I raised my hand for *Amelia Earhart* because the life of a woman pilot had to be full of adventure, but Miss Hadley gave it to Sharon Judson, who was afraid of bees, thunder, and the machine the school nurse used to test our hearing.

Finally, there were only two books left. "Who still doesn't have a biography?" she asked.

I raised my hand. Eddie Wagner flicked his wrist.

The two books left were *Luther Burbank* and *George Washington Carver*.

"By coincidence, these two are both about men who experimented with plants," Miss Hadley said. "Burbank developed many unusual varieties of fruit, like the pomato and the plumcot, and he is famous for his beautiful Shasta daisies. Carver invented more than three hundred products made from peanuts."

Eddie looked out the window.

"Lee?" Miss Hadley held both books out.

I liked the idea of plumcots and pomatoes. I was already thinking up new vegetable varieties like squashrooms and beancumbers. I reached for *Luther Burbank*.

Suddenly, a hand crossed in front of mine. Eddie wrapped his fingers around the book.

Miss Hadley kept her grip on it, too. "Eddie, you can't have this book unless you promise that you are going to read it."

Eddie stared at a place behind her as if he hadn't heard.

Miss Hadley began to draw *Luther Burbank* toward her. I shifted in my seat and held out my hand for it.

"Okay," Eddie grunted.

Miss Hadley sighed—but she let him have the book. I couldn't believe it! I was sure Eddie didn't care spit about fruit or flowers. Didn't she know he'd only grabbed that book because I'd wanted it?

"Lee, I think you'll find Mr. Carver had an amazing life," she said, turning to me. "He was born a slave and was orphaned as an infant. Yet he grew up to be a world-renowned scientist and a professor." She set the last book on my desk.

I let it sit there without touching it. It wasn't fair—I should have gotten *Luther Burbank*.

Miss Hadley sighed again. She gave my shoulder the softest pat before she returned to the front of the classroom.

As soon as her back was turned, Eddie leaned across the aisle toward me. "Biographies," he whispered, "are bullcrud."

7

After school I ran right home. But instead of going upstairs, I headed for the basement to have a look at the bike Zeke had offered me. I figured I could just *borrow* it whenever I wanted to take a ride. I'd told myself that there was a difference between a gift and a loan, so I wouldn't actually be disobeying my mother. Not that I planned to tell her about it, anyway.

"Zeke?" I called as I entered the dimly lit basement.

The door to the bike and carriage room swung open. "Right here," Zeke said. He had on his leather work gloves, and there was a trickle of sweat at his temple, even though the basement was chilly. He pushed a trash can full of old wheels and broken spokes against the door to keep it open. "The one I found for you is over there."

I followed his finger past the trikes, two-wheelers, strollers, and prams. "The blue one?" I squeaked as I eyed a streamlined English racer with narrow wheels, a pearly blue frame, and hand brakes. It was a real beauty.

"No, the red one." Zeke squeezed down a narrow row and stopped at an older model—little-kid red with fat tires. I knew the simple handlebars meant it had foot brakes.

I wondered who owned the fancy racer—I didn't remember ever seeing anyone riding it. But I didn't ask. I didn't want Zeke to think I was ungrateful.

I took a deep breath and coughed. "Zeke? If it's okay with you, I'll just borrow the bike. I don't want to keep it."

I crossed my fingers, hoping he wouldn't ask why not, but Zeke only said, "Sure, Lee. Borrow it as often as you like."

"Okay, thanks. I'll take good care of it," I promised.

As I wheeled the bike out of the alley, I heard someone calling me. "Hey, Wormhead, you have a flat tire." It was Gary, one of the twins who lived on the second floor of the building.

"Yeah, Wormhead. Where'd you get that bike—the junkyard?" his brother Larry added.

Wormhead was their nickname for me because of my brown, curly hair. Some people thought my mop of ringlets came from a permanent wave. But I never would have let Mom give me one of those things. I hated my hair, although Deb used to say it made me look like Annette, the most popular girl on the *Mickey Mouse Club* show.

"Shut up, Cheesebrains!" I said, without stopping. I knew my tires weren't flat.

"What do you want to ride that old wreck for? Don't you want to play Monkey in the Middle?" Gary asked. A pink rubber ball whizzed over my head.

On the other side of me, Larry caught it. "Yeah, come on! Leave that wreck for the garbageman." The ball passed in front of my nose this time, but I still ignored it. Gary and Larry didn't have bikes—or need them. They were in sixth grade like me, but ever since their father died, their mother had made them stay on our block. I guess she was afraid something would happen to them, too.

I walked the bike to the corner and crossed the street. Then I went straight for another block before I turned down a side street. It was one I didn't know very well, which was exactly what I needed. It had been a long time since I'd been bicycling.

I stayed on the sidewalk, pedaling slowly, trying to find my balance. It was hard to keep the handlebars from jiggling back and forth. The fat tires bounced over every crack and bump. I nearly fell several times, but I managed to keep on going.

I was passing a row of small private houses that looked alike—crumbling driveways and peeling paint—when a skinny orange cat ran in front of me. I swerved as the cat yowled in surprise. The next thing I knew, I was sprawled on the ground.

"You okay?"

I looked up and saw Eddie Wagner. For once, his clammed-up face actually looked surprised. I hated him seeing me on my hands and knees like I was some little baby.

"I'm fine," I said, though my scraped palms throbbed as I pushed myself up.

"You learning how to ride?" Eddie cracked a half-smile as if he thought that idea was funny.

"No! I'm just a little rusty." I looked across the street to where the scrawny cat was crouched under a shrub. "That cat surprised me and I fell."

"Stupid cat." Eddie picked up a pebble and threw it at the animal. "Scat, Reject!" The creature dove under a parked car.

"Hey, don't!" I protested. "It wasn't the cat's fault."

"So?" Eddie picked up another stone and pitched it, but it only bounced off the rear tire.

Underneath the car, the cat sat and licked a paw. "Is that cat yours?" I asked.

"Reject is nobody's cat," Eddie answered, turning his back on the animal. "Who'd want him?"

"No one, I guess. He's really ugly." The truth was, I would have loved to have a cat. I was sure if I brushed that scruffy orange fur and fed him some of Mom's leftovers, Reject would have looked fine in no time. I would have named him, too—maybe Oopsy or Rusty. But there wasn't any room for a cat at our place.

I grabbed the handlebars and pulled the bike upright. "See you," I said.

"Whatsa matter? Afraid to ride?"

"No." Without looking back at Eddie, I got on and pushed off slowly.

"Hey, Skippy—if you pedal faster, you won't wobble so much," Eddie called.

"M.Y.O.B., *Booknapper*," I shouted back, but I gripped the handlebars tighter in my sore palms and pumped my legs. The bike moved faster. The ride was smoother.

"Still too slow!" Eddie shouted as I turned the corner.

By the time I reached the Burkes' house, my riding

was better. But there was no one on the porch to see it. "Polly?" I called, in case she was behind the rose trellis.

No one answered. I scanned the fence. The note I'd left in the morning was gone. I wondered if Polly had found it, or if someone else had taken it. I parked my bike on the sidewalk and walked through the open gate and up the porch steps. But although I rang the bell twice, no one came.

Finally, I gave up. I'd wanted Polly to see my new bike, even if it wasn't much to look at. I'd thought maybe we could go riding together.

I got back on the seat and was about to push off when I noticed something. A rolled-up sheet of pale blue paper was tucked beneath the handle of the gate. I snatched it out and smoothed it flat.

Dear Lee,
Please come at ten A.M. on Saturday (tomorrow!) for tea and a game of Parcheesi with Eileen, Timmy, and me.
Your friend,
Polly

8

For a moment, I was surprised when Aunt Bea opened the door to our apartment. Then I threw my arms around her. "I almost forgot it was Friday night!" I exclaimed as I breathed in her sweet apple smell.

"Forgot? You must have been doing something very exciting," she said as she kissed me on each cheek. "Ooh, your face is warm."

I wished I could tell her about the bike. But I only said, "I ran all the way up the stairs."

We went into the kitchen, where Mom was making chicken soup. As usual, Aunt Bea's special apple cake was sitting on the counter. Besides being sisters, my mother and Aunt Bea were best friends. They'd come to America when they were girls. For as long as I could remember, they'd talked on the telephone every day. And every Friday, Aunt Bea and Uncle Harold came over for supper.

"Hi, Mom," I said as I gave my mother a kiss.

She gave me her softest, happiest smile. I knew Mom was younger than most kids' mothers. But around Aunt Bea her face seemed to become even more youthful—almost like a girl's. "Here, taste." She held out a spoonful of soup for me. "You're just in time to set the table."

I tried the salty golden broth. "Yummy," I told her. "I'll just go to the bathroom and wash my hands."

In the living room, Dad and Uncle Harold were watching the news with Mikey sitting between them on the sofa.

"Do you think this country is ready to elect a Roman Catholic president?" I heard my father ask.

Uncle Harold made a sound that was like a grumble and a sigh together. "It's going to be tough. Kennedy's not just Catholic, he's young—the same age as you." Uncle Harold clapped my father on the shoulder. "A lot is going to depend on how he does in the debates. We'll have a better idea next week after the first one."

In school, we'd talked about the presidential election coming in November. Miss Hadley was planning to let us hold a vote in our classroom. I'd been thinking of choosing Kennedy because he was a real war hero. Besides, he was so handsome.

Dad noticed me lingering in the doorway. "No kisses for the men?" he called. I ran in and gave each of them a peck. It was funny how it could feel like we were a big family, even though there were only six of us.

At dinner, Dad and Uncle Harold got into a sort of contest about who had the harder job when they were boys.

"I was a shoeshine boy—" Dad began.

"So? What's so hard?" Uncle Harold interrupted.

Dad wiped his mouth with his napkin. "My customers were so poor and their shoes were so thin that sometimes I polished holes in the toes. Then I had to pay *them!*"

I burst out laughing. Mikey laughed, too, even though he didn't understand what Dad had said. Mom and Aunt Bea looked at each other and shook their heads, but they were giggling like teenagers.

"So?" Uncle Harold said. "I was a rag collector."

My father winked at me. "So? What's so hard?"

"The rags were very tricky to get—because, at the time, most people were wearing them."

We all started laughing again, even Dad.

Then Uncle Harold asked me the same question he did every week. "What's new in school?"

I thought for a moment. "We're reading biographies. I got *George Washington Carver*."

"Carver was the peanut man," Uncle Harold said.

Great. I could already imagine the kids in my class calling me Peanut Girl. "I think he knew about more than peanuts," I said. "The jacket on my book says even though he wasn't allowed to go to school in his town when he was a kid, he became a world-famous plant scientist when he grew up."

"Why couldn't he go to school?" Mom asked.

"Because in those days it was only for white kids, and he was Negro."

"Mmm," Mom answered as if she wasn't really listening. Then she passed the bread around. It was funny, but I felt a little hurt. Usually, she was interested in anything I was studying in school.

"In many places down south, the schools are still segregated," Uncle Harold told me. "That means that there are separate facilities for Negroes and whites— hospitals, movie theaters, buses, parks—even bathrooms and water fountains. But people have begun to challenge the idea."

While I ate, I tried to imagine how I would feel

if I wasn't allowed to go to the park or the movies in my neighborhood, or even to P.S. 119. But it was scary. I made myself think of something else.

"Polly Burke invited me over for tea and Parcheesi tomorrow. Is it okay if I go?" I could feel myself grinning what Uncle Harold calls my hundred-watt smile.

Mom didn't smile back. Not even a twenty-five-watt one. "You don't like tea. The last time you were sick, I had to put in half a jar of honey before you'd drink it."

"I don't care about the tea. I want to play Parcheesi." I didn't admit I thought board games were boring. I was hoping when we finished the game, we could have another shipwreck.

"What about Mikey's walk?" Mom reminded me. After lunch on Saturdays it was my job to wheel my brother around the neighborhood in his stroller until he fell asleep.

"I want to go, Mom. There's nothing to do around here." I looked around the table. Everyone was bent over, clinking and slurping.

"What about that big dollhouse? It's taking up a lot of space. If you're not going to play with it, maybe we should give it away."

"No!" I shouted.

Mom dropped her spoon. Soup splashed onto the tablecloth.

I shoved my chair back and went to get another napkin to blot up the spill.

"Maybe the game doesn't take so long to play," Aunt Bea said when I came back to the table.

"It doesn't," I answered. I looked at my mother. "I'll be back by lunchtime—promise."

"Ssss," my mother sighed like a punctured balloon. "All right, go play Parcheesi. But be careful."

"Careful of what?" I murmured under my breath. Lately, it felt like she had an objection to everything I wanted to do. I was beginning to feel like Rapunzel of Brooklyn, stuck in a fourth-floor apartment instead of a tower.

Dear Deb,

I guess you've been too busy to write. Your new seventh-grade friends probably know the words to all of Elvis's songs and which color lipstick goes best with your eyes. Probably, you're taking French, just like you always wanted. I wish I could speak French so I could talk without Mom knowing what I was saying—except I don't know anyone who'd understand me.

I am invited to play Parcheesi at the home of my new friend, Polly Burke, tomorrow. I think you would like

Polly because she is very sophisticated. She is serving tea, which you know I hate, but I'm going anyway.

Mikey is teething again. He bit a dent in Mrs. Weenie's head when I wasn't looking. The Weenies still miss you!

Your friend, I hope (ha!),

Lee

9

You're here!" Polly sang when she opened the door. "We've been waiting for you. Come on in, we're playing in the parlor."

I knew the word *parlor* from the kiddie rhyme "'Come into my parlor,' said the spider to the fly," but I'd never actually been in one. It didn't look much different from a fancy living room. There was a red velvet sofa, some chairs, a table, and a rug patterned with birds and flowers. The Parcheesi board was on the table. At each corner of the board was a delicate cup brimming with tea.

"Hi, Lee," Eileen said, looking over a cup painted with tiny blue violets. "Sit here—we already set up the red playing pieces for you." She pointed to the chair on her right.

"Your teacup's the one with the red roses on it," Timmy added.

"Okay." I pulled out my chair, careful not to bump the table.

Polly sat opposite me. "We decided to let you be first. Go ahead—shake the dice cup."

An alarm like the fire bell at school began gonging inside my head. I wondered why they were letting me be red when everyone always wanted the red playing pieces. And why was I going first? Then I thought of something else. Why were Eileen and Timmy there before me? I was sure I'd come on time. I'd been watching the clock since I got up hours ago.

I shook the dice cup and spilled the little cubes onto the board. "Seven—I get to move a man out," I said.

"Lucky!" Polly exclaimed. She picked up her cup, which had yellow daisies, and slurped loudly. "Mmm . . . good tea."

Eileen lifted her cup and took a sip. "Yes. It's as sweet as angels' breath. Did you use honey or sugar?"

"Both."

"It's so yummy. Taste it, Tim," Eileen ordered.

Timmy just stared into his cup.

"My turn." Eileen reached for the dice cup. "I always drink tea on Saturdays to relax," she said between shakes. Her pale, plump hand moved so slowly, it looked like she might fall asleep on the game board.

"Mmmm, me, too." Polly took a long sip and looked at me. "Why don't you drink yours before it gets cold, Lee?"

"Yes! There's nothing ickier than cold tea." Eileen nodded her head up and down like a horse.

Did they really think I was dumb enough not to know they were up to something? I wondered what they had put in my cup. Toothpaste? Hot pepper? There was only one way to find out.

I picked up my cup and gulped the whole thing down so fast that I didn't even taste it.

"Eeee!" Eileen gasped.

"Jesus Beezus," Timmy whispered. Eileen didn't even scold him.

In my head, I counted to twenty. Then I stood up. "I feel sick," I moaned. I clutched my stomach and dropped slowly to my knees. "Ooooh! Ugh!" I flopped onto my side, rolled onto my back, and fluttered my eyes a few times before I shut them.

"We've killed her! We've killed her!" Eileen cried. "You said she wouldn't drink the whole thing."

"I thought she'd just take a little sip," Polly answered. "There must be something wrong with her taste buds."

"Oh, why did I ever listen to you?" Eileen wailed. "Come quick, Timmy! Let's go home."

"You can't just leave me here with the body," Polly protested. "Besides, she might not be dead. Maybe we should call an ambulance."

"No, no! We can't let anyone find out. My mother will kill me," Eileen shouted. "Tim, come on!"

"I'll tell everyone it was your idea," Polly threatened.

"I only put in the salt. You put in the bubble bath!"

"What about the toilet water? You added that."

"You dropped in the ground-up chalk."

"You put in the dead ant."

"You added the pinch of goldfish food."

"It was your brother that stuck in his earwax!"

Fish food? Earwax? I nearly gagged.

"She might be in hell," Timmy whispered. "Robby Donovan says that's where Jews go."

I nearly sat up and shouted, "No we don't! Jews don't even believe in hell," because that's what my mother told me. Back in kindergarten, an older girl had announced that if you said curses you'd go to hell, which really worried me because sometimes when Dad was mad, he said "Damn it!" and "Craps!" But Mom's words had washed my worries away. Kindergartners think their mothers are always right.

Just before I gave up playing dead, Polly snapped, "That's a bunch of junk! If every sinner or non-believer went to hell, there'd be no one in heaven but saints. Your own mother would be going to the devil."

"She would not!" Eileen shrieked.

"She drinks, doesn't she? My mother says that's why she totters when she walks."

"That's a lie! My mom just gets dizzy because something's wrong with her ears. And if you don't take that back, I'm going home."

"Okay, okay, I take it back. I'm sorry. Anyway, if we've killed Lee, we'll all be going to hell. We'd better check for signs of life."

I heard Polly drop to her knees. As she bent over me, one of her feathery braids tickled my nose and nearly drove me crazy. Next, my arm was lifted up. I concentrated on keeping it floppy, even when it was released. As my funny bone hit the floor, I had to stifle a giant "ouch."

"Yep, she's dead," Polly said in a voice no different than she'd say, "Yep, it's Saturday." I was so insulted that I nearly jumped up and walked out. But then I heard her start sniffling. "It's so sad! I was sure we were going to become best friends. Come on, we'll have to bury her. You two go dig a hole in the yard. I'll write the funeral service."

Best friends? I decided to stay dead awhile longer.

"Oh no! Bury your *best friend* yourself," Eileen sputtered. "Timmy and I are leaving."

"Wait! You can't go! It's not fair!" Polly scrambled after them.

"Fair, shmare, I don't care," Eileen chanted. The door slammed.

I opened my eyes and peeked. When I saw the room was empty, I scrambled up, grabbed a copy of *Life* magazine, and made myself comfortable on the sofa. In another moment, Polly came racing back.

"I knew it! I could feel you breathing," she said when she saw me.

I made a clucking noise the way my mother did when she disapproved of something. "That Eileen sure is a fair-weather friend." I started giggling. "Do you think she really believed I was dead?"

Polly cradled her cheek in her palm. "Ummm, I'm not sure. Eileen's afraid of practically everything. I don't think she'd stay in the same room with a real dead body. She'd be too worried about ghosts."

"Oh." I took a deep breath. There was something I wanted to ask. "Is Eileen your best friend?"

Polly smiled at me. "I don't have a best friend yet—but I think I'm going to have one soon."

I felt like I'd just gone to heaven, although I wasn't sure if Jews believed in that either.

Suddenly, I remembered Mikey's walk. "I've got to go home and take my baby brother out in his stroller. Do you want to come with me?"

"You have a baby brother? You're so lucky!" Polly held up her wrist and checked her Cinderella watch. "I can't go now. My mother's coming back for lunch. She expects me to be here."

"That's okay. I understand about mothers," I said. I was actually kind of relieved. I hardly ever brought anyone home to play. Our place was so small, Mom could hear every word anyone said.

I started for the vestibule, but Polly put her hand on my shoulder. "You could come here for Sunday dinner tomorrow. We get home from church at twelve. Afterward, we'll have the whole afternoon together."

Dinner at lunchtime? It sounded so formal. Did Polly's family pray before they ate? I wondered. Would I have to bow my head? Should I keep my eyes open or closed? I was worried that I wouldn't know how to act, but I wanted to go back to the attic. I wanted to have shipwrecks and fight pirates. I wanted a best friend.

"Okay," I agreed. "I'll ask if I can."

10

"Spell *Cheyenne*," Mom said while she spooned the last bit of vanilla pudding into Mikey's open mouth.

"C-h-e-y-e-n-n-e." Spelling was my best subject. I only had to look at the list of words Miss Hadley gave us each week, and poof!—it was memorized. But Mom still liked to quiz me. In a way, I think she was really testing herself. She had to quit school after tenth grade because she needed to go to work. Once, she told me, she wanted to be a teacher.

"Capital cities is a dumb idea for a spelling test," I complained. "I don't see why I need to know about some place in Wyoming."

"You never know where you'll find yourself one day," Mom answered. "It's good to be prepared." She looked out the window as if she were checking to see where she was right now.

I stood behind her chair and rested my chin on her head. "I think we're still in Brooklyn, Mom. I don't see any cowboys or cattle."

She pointed a long, slender finger. "Isn't that an Indian chief on that horse over there?"

"Where?" When I craned my neck for a better look, she reached up and tickled me.

"Stop!" I giggled, not really meaning it. I loved when Mom got silly. I knew I should ask about going to Polly's now while she was still feeling happy. Her moods could change pretty quickly.

I reached for her hand and began playing with her fingers. "Mom, could I go to Polly Burke's for Sunday dinner tomorrow?"

She raised her eyebrows. "Again? You were just there."

"I like Polly. She's really nice." I gripped Mom's hand a little tighter.

"We're going out for Chinese. You'll miss it." One Sunday a month, our family ate at the Mandarin Teapot with Aunt Bea and Uncle Harold.

"I don't care," I answered, but my belly grumbled as if it insisted upon speaking for itself.

"People like the Burkes eat things from cans," Mom said, pulling her fingers from mine. "They have fancy names, but who knows what's really in them?

Chopped horses or pigeons, maybe. You'll get a stomachache."

People like the Burkes. I knew what my mother really meant was "people who weren't Jewish." Sometimes, when she was on the phone with Aunt Bea, she called them *the goyim.* That name made my stomach hurt, but I didn't say so. Mom was the one who got aches when she was upset.

"Polly eats that food and she's not sick," I said.

"That's because she's used to it."

"Owwwwt!" Mikey suddenly demanded, squirming in his high chair. He threw his bottle on the floor. When it was time for his nap, he always got fussy. But maybe he didn't like the sound of our voices.

Mom stood up and lifted him out. "Sunday is a special day for *them.* Are you sure you're welcome?"

I bent down and picked up the baby's bottle. "Yes," I said, but I was suddenly doubtful. I almost wished she would just say no.

"Let her go, Ruthie," my father said from behind his newspaper. "Lee should have all kinds of friends. It's important to see how other people live."

I looked at him, amazed that he was even listening.

"Ba-bye! Ba-bye!" Mikey shrieked.

I went to get his sweater from the dresser we shared. Aunt Bea had knitted him one like mine, cheery red with a pointy hood. When I returned, my mother said, "All right. Eat Sunday dinner with the Burkes. See how *the goyim* live."

In the pit of my stomach, I felt anger begin rising, making my body get all tight and trembly. But before it reached my throat, I felt a little squeeze at my elbow.

I turned around and looked into Dad's eyes. His head gave the tiniest shake no. Then he smiled at me, and the angry feeling began to fade.

11

"Hey, Wormhead, want to play Monkey in the Middle?" Larry asked as I struggled to get Mikey's stroller through the front door.

"Can't you see I'm busy, Cheesebrain?" I pushed the stroller harder than I'd meant to, and Mikey jerked backward. He laughed as if he thought it was a game.

"How about you, Mikey?" Gary said, when I finally had the stroller on the sidewalk. He crouched down in front of my brother. "You want to play?"

"Gooey!" Mikey said, holding up the stuffed yellow dog he always took to sleep with him.

"Oh, Gooey wants to play?" Gary took the toy dog from Mikey's outstretched hands. "Okay."

"Give it back!" I snapped. But Gary threw Gooey over my head, straight to Larry.

"Looks like you're the monkey after all, Wormhead," he jeered. "Eee! Eee!" Larry curled his arms under and scratched at his armpits.

In his stroller, Mikey chuckled with delight. "Eee-eee! Eee-eee!" he squealed.

"Cut it out, Mikey," I grumbled. "Whose side are you on?"

"Hey, Mikey, want to see Gooey do a pop-up?" Gary called. "Watch!" He threw Gooey up high.

My brother laughed a real belly laugh as the floppy-eared dog disappeared into the leaves of the big oak tree in front of our building. "Don't be a cheesebrain, too, Mikey," I hissed.

Larry rushed forward to catch Gooey again. But Gooey didn't come down.

"Uh-oh, Gooey's stuck on a branch." Gary shaded his eyes as he peered up through the leaves.

"I can see that for myself," I snapped. "You'd better get him down."

Mikey's eyes were bright as he looked up. "Gooey! Gooey! Gooey!" he chanted.

"Don't worry, Mikey. Watch this." Gary pulled a pink rubber ball out of his pocket. He squinted up at the tree for a moment. Then he threw. And missed.

"Goooooey! Goooooey!" Mikey's voice had the frantic pitch of an ambulance siren. In another minute, he'd be crying.

Suddenly, out of the corner of my eye, I saw something sail through the air and disappear into the oak leaves. In a second, Gooey dropped onto the sidewalk, followed by a rock that was nearly as big as my hand.

I looked around to see where it had come from. Eddie Wagner was stepping out from between the hedges.

"Hey, where'd you come from?" Larry asked.

I kept quiet. I didn't even let my eyes wander toward the hedges.

"You could've killed someone with that rock, you know," Gary said.

I snatched Gooey from the sidewalk and dusted him off. "Say thank you to Eddie," I said, handing the dog to Mikey. But my brother only popped his thumb into his mouth and rubbed Gooey against his cheek.

Eddie pushed his hair out of his hard, flat eyes. I might have said thank you myself if he hadn't looked so mean—like his scowl was carved into his face. Without a word, he scooped up the rock and stuffed it into his pocket. Then he began walking away.

"Where d'ya think he got a rock like that? There are only pebbles around here," Larry said when Eddie was halfway down the block.

"He was probably saving it to break a window.

Haven't you noticed some of the little basement ones are cracked?" Gary answered.

"That's not fair!" I said in a hushed voice, because Mikey had fallen asleep.

Gary pushed a fat finger into my middle. "Oh yeah? Well, I've seen Eddie hanging around the building a bunch of times, Wormhead. What do you think he was carrying that rock for?"

I shoved his hand away. "You can't prove anything!" I didn't have any idea why I was so mad. I hated Eddie.

"What are you, his lawyer?"

I ignored the remark and began pushing my sleeping brother along Avenue J. But I couldn't stop thinking about Eddie. Just last week, I'd seen the janitor at school replacing a cracked pane of glass in the secretary's office. I hadn't thought about how it had gotten that way.

And another thing about Eddie—he was definitely a sneak. It looked like he'd discovered another one of my hiding places. Had he been spying on me?

Suddenly I remembered Teena Weenie. I'd left her in the electrical box! I began pushing the stroller more quickly. Then I began running with it. When I pushed the stroller over a curb, Mikey opened his eyes. I held my breath and rocked it for a minute, and his eyes fluttered closed again.

As soon as I turned down the block toward school, I began squinting. I could see the traffic-light pole and the electrical box. The door looked shut. It *was* shut. I took a deep breath and slowed down a little.

"Time to go home, Teena," I murmured as I tried to open the little door. But it was shut so tightly I couldn't budge it. I fit my fingernails in the crack so I could pry it open. But the door appeared to be jammed. Someone must have been fooling with it, I realized. What if they had taken Teena? Tears sprang to my eyes.

I looked around in the gutter for something to use on the door. There were some leaves, twigs, and a rock. I wondered if I should try smashing the box open, but I was afraid someone might see me and call the police. Besides, I'd probably just jam the door worse.

I picked up the smallest twig I could find and worked it around the edges. I guess I was pressing too hard, because the twig got caught in the crack. When I jerked it out again, the door popped open. And there was Teena. I grabbed her out and kissed her on her little plastic head. I didn't even care if anyone saw.

12

Sitting at the Burkes' dining room table made me wish I'd listened to my mother. Twice already, my napkin had drifted off my lap. Each time I bent to retrieve it, I could feel Mrs. Burke's birdy eyes following me as if I were a plump, juicy worm she was thinking of eating.

The food on my plate didn't look like anything my mother had ever served me. It had a fancy name, chicken à la king, and it was covered with a snowy white sauce. I dipped my fork into it and licked the tip. It was smooth and didn't have much taste, which was okay with me. Mom's cooking was salty and spicy and could make you belch. Wait till I told her how elegant Mrs. Burke's dinner was.

I speared a chunk of meat on my fork and popped it in my mouth. When I bit down, the chicken resisted. I chewed harder, but my teeth didn't seem to be working. I couldn't flatten the chunk enough to swallow. In fact, it felt like it was growing bigger.

With my tongue, I pushed the meat into the pocket of my cheek and reached for the glass at my place. Mrs. Burke had poured milk for me without asking if I'd prefer water. At home, I refused to drink milk unless it had chocolate syrup in it. My mother, I knew, would be amazed to see me now.

I drank almost the entire glass as I tried to wash the lump down. Gulping the milk helped move the chicken to the back of my throat—but that was where it stopped. To my horror, I made a gagging sound as I forced it the rest of the way.

"Lee, are you okay?" Polly asked.

"Yes," I croaked.

"Seems like this chicken's still got some fight in it," Mr. Burke joked. He held his fork like a weapon and stabbed at a chunk. "Down, girl! Down!"

When Polly started giggling, I let myself join in. We each speared the next bite as if we were stalking a live bird. But when I put the chicken in my mouth, my mother's warning came back to me. Maybe this wasn't really chicken . . . maybe it was pigeon.

I clamped my teeth down to keep from gagging again. Pigeon juice squirted onto my tongue! I could feel tears gathering at the corners of my eyes as I picked up my napkin and pretended to wipe my mouth. While I rubbed, I spit the pigeon into the napkin and bunched it up.

I looked at Polly. She was pushing her food around her plate without eating.

Mr. Burke clunked down his fork, although there was still a lot of bird mess left on his plate. "Olive has invited us to spend Christmas in New Hampshire this year," he announced.

Polly sat up taller in her chair. "Olive is my aunt," she told me. "Her house is on the edge of a forest. She puts pine needles in her pillows so in the morning your hair smells all piney. And her cat always has kittens!"

She turned her head toward her father so fast, her braids spun out like whips. "Maybe Lee could come with us."

Mr. Burke grinned at me. He had the same big, friendly smile as Polly. "I think we might be able to arrange that. Does it sound good to you, Lee?"

Before I could even think about it, Mrs. Burke said, "Oh no, not at Christmas, dear."

"Why, Mom?" Polly asked.

Mrs. Burke busied herself collecting plates.

"Why?" This time Polly kicked a table leg. Milk sloshed over the top.

"Polly!" her mother scolded. "You know the reason perfectly well. And if you don't calm down this instant, I'll send Lee home, and you will go up to your room."

Mr. Burke leaned over and patted my hand. "Some other time, then."

I felt as embarrassed as if I'd asked to be invited to Polly's aunt's house myself. I knew why Mrs. Burke had said no to Polly. It was the same reason my own mother would have given if I'd asked her.

Jewish people don't celebrate Christmas. Mom had said it when I'd wanted to sit on the knee of the Santa at Macy's, when I'd tried to decorate her rubber plant like a Christmas tree, and when I'd been caught hanging a kneesock out on the fire escape one Christmas Eve. Once I got too old to believe in Santa, I quit trying to celebrate. But I still really loved the twinkling lights and Christmas music.

It seemed silly to argue about Christmas now—this was only the last week in September. Besides, I didn't care about going to Polly's aunt's house—it was the attic I was itching to get to.

At least Mrs. Burke's dessert was something I recognized—lime Jell-O. I knew my parents would be having fortune cookies and little cubes of pineapple on toothpicks. I lifted a Jell-O cube with my spoon and closed my eyes, pretending it was a silky, tasty wonton. But when I popped my spoon in my mouth, there was nothing on it. My eyes flew open. I looked at my lap. To my relief, it was still clean.

Then I glanced at the floor. From underneath Mrs. Burke's chair, a neon-green cube glowed and quivered. "Sorry," I said in a voice that came out like a whisper.

Mrs. Burke smiled a closed-mouth smile. "Don't worry about it, dear. But you know, we always keep our eyes open when we eat."

13

Polly's bed had a roof made of pale pink material like a ballerina's skirt. The only place I'd seen such a bed before was in fairy-tale books. On the floor was a fluffy pink rug like I imagined a princess would have. Polly marched right across it and plopped in the middle of her puffy quilt.

"Come on in," she said, bouncing on the mattress. She looked into one of the three mirrors set over the little table opposite the bed. "This vanity table is supposed to be for putting on makeup. But my mother won't even let me use the toilet water Aunt Olive gave me last Christmas." She unscrewed the cap and held the bottle up to my nose. "Here, smell."

But toilet water made me think of the tea—and all the other things Polly, Eileen, and Timmy had put in it. I sat on the edge of the bed and gulped.

"If I tell you a secret, do you promise never to tell anyone?" Polly asked.

"Sure." In the three mirrors, I could see myself smiling hundred-watt smiles.

She pulled out the vanity's center drawer and reached all the way into the back. "Open your palm," she ordered.

I held my hand out flat, and Polly dropped a little circlet of pink and white beads into it. It was a baby bracelet.

"O-L-I-V-E," I said, reading the letters out loud. "Was this your aunt's?"

"No, Olive's my real name," Polly said. She was whispering, even with the door closed. "I'm named for my aunt. I hate it, though. When I grow up, I'm going to have my birth certificate changed to *Polly* officially."

I tried to imagine her as Olive, but all I could think of was Olive Oyl in the Popeye comics. They were both tall and skinny, but Polly wasn't at all silly like the cartoon Olive. "Don't worry," I assured her. "Even if I were forced to eat a whole pigeon, I would never tell anyone."

Polly looked a little surprised, but she leaned

her head closer to mine. "Now you tell me a secret. Then we'll be bound to each other forever."

I considered mentioning my secret hiding places, but the Burkes' house was full of spots a thousand times better than tree roots or electrical boxes. I could tell Polly about the borrowed bike, but I thought only my mother would care about that.

I looked into the vanity mirrors and saw three Pollys staring at me. "Okay," I said finally. "I skipped a grade. Otherwise, I'd be in fifth instead of sixth."

"Why is that a secret?"

I ran my palm back and forth over her quilt. "When kids know you skipped, they treat you like a baby."

"Eileen's in fifth grade. Do you think she's a baby?" Polly turned away from the mirror and looked at the real me.

"No. Of course not."

"Well, neither do I." Polly went fishing in the vanity drawer again. She took out a key on a blue ribbon and dangled it in front of me. "Here's another secret."

"A key? What's it open?"

"The Sunday-school closet. I'm the class monitor. There are bags and bags of Oreos in there." Polly flashed a grin at the mirrors. "Everyone gets two at snack time, but whenever the teacher, Mrs. Dobbs, goes outside for a cigarette break, I take them out again. We all eat as many as we want."

"Doesn't she notice?"

"She never says anything . . ." Polly paused and turned from the mirror to grin at me. ". . . and I never say anything about the cigarettes."

I smiled back, but I was a bit shocked that she would steal from church. I thought it would make God especially mad. Zeke's wife, Mary Mayfield, called her church a house of God. If Polly's church was also one of God's houses, wouldn't He expect everyone who came there to be on their best behavior?

My family never went to synagogue. Dad said it was because Mom was angry with God. He told me if I wanted to talk to God, I could do it anywhere. But it worried me a little that I never spoke to God in an official place. When Mom went to the hospital to have the baby, I'd asked God to please let her be okay and to make the baby a girl. But I didn't go to a synagogue—I just lay in bed and asked. Mom came back fine, but she brought home my brother, so I couldn't be sure if God had heard me or not.

From the vanity, Polly extracted two unsharpened pencils and offered one to me. She began puffing furiously on the eraser end of hers. I inhaled noisily and pretended I was blowing big, gray smoke rings. Then we both got the same idea—coughing. We hacked and hacked, until Mrs. Burke called up the stairs. "Polly? Is someone sick?"

"No, Mom, we're fine." We stifled our giggles into pillows. When we stopped, Polly said, "Now, you tell me another secret."

I pressed my palm to my forehead. After a few seconds, I said, "I don't think I have any more."

"There must be something."

"There is, sort of. But I shouldn't—I mean, it's not exactly mine."

Polly cocked her head and waited.

I felt a pang of guilt before I even said the words—"My mother is an orphan."

"I don't think grown-ups can be orphans." Polly fingered the end of her braid.

"I mean, when she was a girl. She was born in Poland, but her parents sent her and her sister to America when Mom was eleven and Bea, my aunt, was fifteen. They were supposed to stay with an old uncle until their parents could get here, but after a year, the uncle died. So they were all alone in America."

"Oh, that's so awful." Polly laid her hand on my arm.

"Yeah." I suddenly had to clear my throat.

"What happened to the girls then?"

"They got put in an orphanage until Bea turned eighteen and could care for the two of them. That's why I said my mom was an orphan."

"But what about her parents? Didn't they come to get the girls?"

"No. They died before they could come here."

Soon after my grandparents sent Mom and Aunt Bea away, their house had been burned down. They hadn't gotten out in time. I'd never told anyone about it except Deb. I hadn't even found out the whole story myself until last year. Before that, when I'd asked Mom where my grandparents were, she'd told me they'd stayed in Poland. If I tried to ask why they never came to America to visit us, she just snapped, "Because they can't!" It was Aunt Bea who'd finally told me the truth.

For a few moments, Polly and I were as quiet as if we were standing at my grandparents' graves. Then Polly glanced at her watch. "Oops! It's almost time for my flying lesson."

"Your what?" I wasn't sure I'd heard her right.

But she only put a finger to her lips and motioned me out of her room. In another moment, we were racing up to the attic.

14

First we have to practice taking off," Polly said as she arranged the blue cushions into an island on the floor. "Here, help me turn this couch around." The floor creaked and groaned as we pushed the heavy thing so the back was facing toward the middle of the room.

Polly kicked off her sneakers and climbed up. "I'm thinking about butterflies and blue jays," she said, wobbling only a little on the narrow edge of the couch's back. "That's what you do when you want to fly."

The island of cushions looked awfully far away from her. I hoped she wasn't going to crack her skull on the wood floor. I kept quiet as she bent her knees and flung herself through a shaft of sunlight that crossed the room. Her arms, legs, and braids flopped like an old rag doll's when she landed.

I ran over to help her up. "Wow! That was really great."

"Thanks. I've been practicing every night." Polly took my hand, and I pulled her up.

I tried to imagine being in the attic at night, alone except for empty, sorry Sir Beetlebug. I didn't even like going into the basement if Zeke wasn't there.

"Okay, your turn," Polly said.

I pulled off my sneakers while she pushed the cushions tighter together. For as long as I could remember, I'd dreamed about flying. At first, I'd be scared as I leaped out of my bedroom window and plunged down toward Avenue J. Then, just as I was about to crash, my body would become light and tingly, and I'd soar up in the air. It was the most wonderful feeling—like being the wind or a shooting star.

I climbed onto the sofa back. I had to curl my toes over the edge to keep from sliding right off. The instant I found my balance, I sprang. The floor, the cushions, and Polly were all one soft blur of color and shape. I heard a faint shriek that sounded like my own voice. Then my heels hit the cushions and I fell over backward.

"Oops—are you okay?" Polly asked.

"Sure." My elbows and rear end were throbbing, but I couldn't wait to try it again.

We took off over and over, until Polly thought we were ready to move on to flying. "We have to start by running," she explained. "Follow me."

We slid across the bare floor in our socks, flapping our arms like wings. It was a little like skating, but also like something that felt freer. Suddenly, Polly shouted, "Look down! We're doing it! WE'RE FLYING!"

We took turns pointing out forests, rivers, and mountains below us. We soared through chains of puffy clouds. We joined flocks of birds that sang to us as we flew. Sometimes a gust of wind blew us faster ahead. Other times, it pushed us backward and made our arms into windmills. Once we got whirled around in a passing tornado.

When we finally grew tired, we landed on our blue island and plopped down to rest. The hair at the back of my neck was damp. Polly was breathing with her mouth open like a dog.

I glanced at her wristwatch. It was a little before five. "I should go," I said.

"In a minute." Polly rose up on her elbows. "One more secret."

"What?" I was already pulling my sneakers back on.

"Not what, *who*—*who's* been teaching me to fly."

Something in her voice made me stop tying a shoelace and look at her. "Okay, who?"

"Peter Pan—he was in my room last night."

I thought for a moment. "Oh, you dreamed it," I said.

Polly shook her head. "Uh-uh."

"You mean you watched *Peter Pan* on TV? I saw it last year." I loved the story of Peter Pan, who could fly and who lived with his pack of Lost Boys on an island called Neverland without any parents. It wasn't sad because their parents weren't dead. The boys had just decided to live with Peter instead, because then they never had to grow up. They got to spend every day having adventures with pirates and Indians.

Polly took off her glasses and rubbed at a speck. Not the TV Peter, *the real Peter*." She sounded kind of offended.

"I wish there were a real Peter. I'd go to Neverland with him in a minute if I didn't have to do my home-work," I joked.

Polly didn't smile. "There *is* a real Peter. I saw his shadow on the wall right next to my vanity table."

"Oh, a shadow." I went back to tying my laces.

"Not just a shadow—*Peter Pan's shadow*." Polly turned away from me and gazed out the window. I couldn't resist looking, too. The sky was the bluish gray of early evening—the exact color of Polly's eyes. But the only thing I saw flying out there was a blackbird.

"I have to go home now." I didn't want to call her a liar, but I also didn't want her to get the idea I'd believe just anything she said. I stood up and began putting the cushions back. "Come on. I'll help you turn the couch around."

Silently, we pushed the furniture back in place. My hand was on the attic door when Polly said softly, "You can't really learn to fly if you don't believe in him, Lee."

I opened the door without answering and edged past Sir Beetlebug.

Mrs. Burke must have heard us running down the stairs because she came into the vestibule as I was getting into my red sweater. "Polly, would you run back up and get my sewing box?"

"Sure, Mom." Polly tapped me lightly on the arm. "Bye, Lee. See you soon."

"Thanks for dinner, Mrs. Burke," I said. I thought she would go back into the kitchen, but she stood there watching me button my sweater.

"I hope you enjoyed it, Lee."

"Um, yes. It was delicious." I wanted to leave, but she was blocking the door. "Well, thanks again."

Mrs. Burke nodded and smiled a closed-mouth

smile that made her lips look stitched together. There wasn't a single wrinkle in her navy skirt. Her white blouse was so starched, it creaked when she moved her arms.

"Okay, I have to go home now. My mom's expecting me."

Mrs. Burke didn't budge. She didn't even act like she'd heard me. I tried to reach around her to grab the doorknob.

"Just a moment, dear." She seized my hand and held it tightly. I started to pull away. Although she looked pale and stringy, Polly's mom had a grip like a dog on a bone. She pushed something into my palm. It felt like paper.

"Take this with you and read it. But don't show it to your mother," she warned. Then she released me.

I stuffed the paper into the pocket of my sweater without looking at it. "I will. I mean, I won't," I mumbled.

Mrs. Burke opened the front door for me. "Give my regards to your parents, dear."

I forced myself to walk down the porch steps and along the green fence. But as soon as I thought Mrs. Burke couldn't see me, I began running. I didn't stop until I got to the hedges that surrounded my building.

Squeezed into the spot that no one knew about, except maybe Eddie, I flattened out the thin, white sheet Mrs. Burke had given me. The handwriting on it was tight and cramped. I could almost see Mrs. Burke's fingers twisted around the pen.

Accept Jesus into your heart before it is too late. The Lord said, suffer the little children who come unto Me. Believe in Him and be saved from the fire that awaits all who turn away.

Here at the fork in the road, you decide your own fate. Walk with the Lord in His sweet, cool meadows and sip of pure, clear waters. Or crawl the parched, rocky landscape of the sinner and nonbeliever, where eternal thirst is answered with fire and ashes.

I had to keep reading the note over and over, because the letters wouldn't hold still. They'd get tiny and faint, and then so big and thick, they all ran together. I tried saying them in my head, but my heart was pounding too loudly to hear. Even so, I knew they meant that something bad was going to happen to me unless I believed in Jesus.

Although I was crouched in my hiding spot, I had the feeling the sky was a giant eyeball looking down at me. In my hand, the paper began trembling. "It's not fair!" I tried to protest. "I'm hardly Jewish. I never even go to synagogue." But all that came out of my throat was a choky sob.

I dug my fingers into the ground around the roots of the hedge and scraped away until I'd made a little hole. Then I stuffed the note into it and covered it back up.

More than anything, I wanted to throw myself into Mom's arms like a baby. I wanted to show her the note and hear her say, "That Mrs. Burke is a crazy one. Don't pay any attention to what she thinks."

But I couldn't. I didn't care about Mrs. Burke's warning not to tell, but I was worried about Mom. If she knew about the note, she might not let me be friends with Polly anymore.

"How was your Sunday dinner?" Mom asked as she opened the door for me.

"Fine."

"We brought home some leftover spareribs for you."

"No, thank you. I'm not hungry." I headed for the bathroom.

"Does your stomach hurt?"

"No! Can't I go to the bathroom without you following me?" I slammed the door and turned on the faucets. For a long time, I stood at the sink and ran warm water over my hands. Then I crept into my room.

Mikey was lying in his crib with a bottle. He was dozing off, but I lifted him out anyway. His warm little body felt so good in my arms, and he was tired enough that he didn't fight being cuddled. I stood there hugging him, swaying back and forth in the darkness until long after he fell back to sleep.

Dear Deb,

Today I went to Polly's for Sunday dinner. We had chicken ala king, which was heavenly. I am going to ask for the recipe so if you ever come to visit, my mother can make it for us.

After we ate, Polly and I went up to her attic to talk about stuff. I guess that's what you've been doing with your friends also—maybe even in French.

One thing I'd like to know is, are your new friends different religions? Polly is Christian and goes to a school that is run by her church. They believe in heaven and hell, which I think is so interesting. What is your opinion of heaven and hell?

Please answer back
Your friend (remember?),
Lee Bloom

15

Later, I brought *George Washington Carver* into the living room and plopped down on the sofa between Mom and Dad. Mom looked up from doing her crossword puzzle, which was her favorite thing next to puttering with her plants.

"Finished your homework?" she asked, reaching out to stroke my curls.

"Yes—except for reading this."

"What made you choose Carver?" Dad asked. His favorite kind of book was a mystery. He actually belonged to a mystery book club and got a new one in the mail every month.

"It was the last one left," I admitted.

"Then George is lucky to have you," my father said.

"Why?"

"Because I'm sure you will treat him with kindness and consideration."

I thought of how I'd really wanted *Luther Burbank*. The way Eddie had grabbed it still burned me up. "It's only a *book*, Dad," I said.

The first part of Carver's life was awfully sad. George was only a tiny baby when he and his mother were kidnapped by slave-stealers. His mother disappeared, but George was found and returned to Mr. and Mrs. Carver—the couple who'd owned his mother. They were nice to him—almost like a family—and they continued raising George after the slaves were freed. But when he was ten, George had to leave home because there wasn't any school for Negro children in Diamond Grove, Missouri, where he lived. More than anything, he wanted to get an education.

When I got to the part where George moved to Kansas to go to a better school, and read how he lived alone in a shack and did white people's laundry to earn money, I had to put the book down. Some white boys in town called George "Washwoman." They were so mean.

"I need some water."

Dad glanced up from his mystery book, but I looked away.

To keep the electric bills down, we lit the kitchen with a night-light after dinner. The tiny bulb always made the room feel weird and unfamiliar. "Probably,

George just had a candle to light his shack," I told myself.

I let the water run in the sink so it would get cold. Out of the corner of my eye, I saw something flit across the wall, just beside the window. When I looked up, it was gone.

My hand trembled as I reached for a glass. I knew I was being silly—Mom and Dad were in the next room. I filled my glass and forced myself to drink slowly. Behind me, I heard a gentle sighing sound. Something soft and fuzzy brushed against my earlobe and made me jump.

For an instant, I saw the shadow of a boy with a feather in his pointed cap. My heart began to thump. When I peeked again, he—the shadow—was gone.

Inside my head, I heard the words Polly had spoken in the attic. *You can't really learn to fly if you don't believe in him.* I hurried back to the living room and threw myself onto the couch between my mother and father. I was worried that they could hear my heart drumming.

Mom looked up. "Everything okay?"

"Yes!" I said, and picked up my book again. But I kept reading the same page over and over without really getting the words.

"It was just a shadow," I murmured as I crawled into bed later. "A friendly one." For once I was glad to have my brother sleeping across the room, even if he was only a baby. As I lay there in the darkness, I barely dared to breathe. Usually I slept on my stomach, but I stayed on my back so I could watch the window. Pretty soon my body grew heavy. If Peter Pan and George Washington Carver had both suddenly appeared, I couldn't have kept my eyes from closing.

In the morning, I remembered flying over a great, gray sea. And when I raised my arms over my head to stretch, they felt kind of sore. Never before had I gotten sore from dreaming. I could hardly wait to go to Polly's after school—though I wasn't sure what to tell her had happened.

16

"I think it would be fun for you to do a project to go along with your book reports," Miss Hadley said as soon as she'd taken attendance.

Perfect Mitchell raised his hand. "What kind of projects?"

"It could be drawing, painting, sewing, woodwork, a diorama, a puzzle—anything you choose." Miss Hadley ticked off each idea on her fingers.

"Could Sandra and I do one together on First Ladies?" Judy Miller asked. She was reading *Martha Washington*, and Sandra Goldstein was reading *Dolley Madison*.

"Group projects are a good idea if you are reading about people who have something in common," Miss Hadley agreed.

I felt my heart shrink. Even if I wanted to do a

group project, there was only one person reading about someone who had anything in common with George Washington Carver.

I let my eyes slip sideways. At the moment, Eddie was sticking a half-sucked cough drop to the underside of his desk. Its cherry-menthol scent hung sickeningly in the air. I tried to imagine what sort of project Eddie would want to do . . . carve a tree out of what was left of his desktop, or steal plants out of other people's gardens, maybe. When he realized I was looking at him, he turned the corners of his mouth down in a smirk. Then he pulled the cough drop off the bottom of his desk and popped it back in his mouth.

I was definitely doing my project alone.

In the afternoon, while I was working on fractions, I couldn't keep from peeking at the classroom clock. I looked at it after I'd converted each fraction, after I'd multiplied it, and after I'd reduced it. I kept thinking about how I'd explain to Polly about what had happened in the kitchen. I remembered she'd glimpsed his shadow on her wall, too.

I was reducing 16/112 when Miss Hadley began rustling papers. Then I heard the sound of tape being ripped from a dispenser. I looked up from my math sheet—everyone did. Some of them groaned. On a corner of the chalkboard, our teacher was hanging up the weekly photo.

"Time for some writing," Miss Hadley announced. "This week's photograph is on a serious subject—discrimination. Earlier this year, in Greensboro, North Carolina, some Negro students were arrested for sitting in at a Woolworth's lunch counter where only white people are permitted to eat. *Sitting in* means staying put when you are ordered to leave, even though you know you will be arrested. It is a nonviolent way of protesting something you think is wrong."

I looked at the picture. Four Negro teenagers were sitting on stools. Behind the counter, the soda jerk in his white cap just stood there staring at them. You could also see some policemen watching them through the store's front window—that gave me the creeps. I thought of how I'd feel if it were me waiting there, never getting served.

Perfect Mitchell's hand flew up. "Why aren't the policemen arresting the soda jerk?"

"The laws in that part of the country are different," Miss Hadley explained. "It's the Negro students who are breaking the law by challenging segregation."

"I would never want to live in a place with unfair

laws," Mitchell said. A lot of the kids murmured in agreement.

For a long moment, Miss Hadley just gazed at us. "If you open your eyes and look around, you'll see that things aren't fair here either," she said in a voice so quiet we leaned forward in our seats.

That made me think about something. I'd been to Woolworth's plenty of times. We had a lot of them in Brooklyn. There was one in our neighborhood that I could walk to, and another that Mom and I always stopped at for orange drinks and frankfurters when we rode the bus downtown to shop. I tried to remember if I'd seen any Negroes at the lunch counters, especially at the downtown one, but I couldn't, which worried me. I didn't think Brooklyn was the kind of place that allowed discrimination, but suddenly I wasn't so sure.

I don't think it's fair that a restaurant could be for white people only. What if George Washington Carver came to eat there? Would they tell him to go away, too? In Diamond Grove, Missouri, where he lived when he was a kid, the school was only for white people. But George wanted an education so badly, he left home to get it. He was only ten years old, but he traveled all by himself to another town where there was a school for Negroes. He didn't have any money or any place to stay. *He didn't know a single person there. But George had a big dream. He wanted to learn everything he could so that someday he could be a teacher or a scientist.*

If it wasn't for George Washington Carver, that lunch counter probably wouldn't have any peanut butter sand-wiches!

17

After school, I hurried to the Burkes'. I was hoping Mrs. Burke wouldn't be there, but the moment I saw Polly on the porch, I forgot to worry. I began waving wildly, the way Perfect Mitchell did when he wanted to answer one of Miss Hadley's questions.

"You'll never guess what happened last night!" I called.

Polly scooted over on the two-seater rocker so I could sit with her. "What happened? Tell me!"

"I think I saw something on our kitchen wall. It looked like the shadow of a boy." The memory of something brushing my ear made me shiver.

Polly nodded solemnly. "Yes, it was Peter. I sent him to warn you. We have to prepare." The way she said it—breathy and secretive—made my skin prickle.

"Prepare for what?" I whispered.

"To defend ourselves. The pirates are coming in

their flying galleon." She leaned over the porch rail and gazed at the sky.

I looked, too, but all I saw was a milky blue blanket like a giant version of the one in Mikey's crib. Together we watched for a while. I thought of mentioning her mother's note. But waiting for pirates seemed so much easier.

"Why are the pirates coming here?"

"To capture us. They need girls to do their cooking and washing. And boys to join their crew."

The only thing I knew how to cook was Rice Krispies and milk. And the only time I'd done the laundry for Mom, I'd put my red socks in with the underwear, and Dad's underpants turned pink. I didn't seem to be the type of girl who would be useful to a pirate crew.

"I didn't actually see Peter Pan," I reminded Polly. "Just a shadow shaped like a boy. It was only there for a second."

"No one can *see* Peter or the pirates. They're invisible except for their shadows. You just have to believe they're there." She jumped up from the rocker. "We've got to surprise them by being able to fight and fly! Let's practice right now. We'll teach Eileen and Timmy, too, but we won't tell them why. You know how worried Eileen always gets."

I got up and followed Polly to the porch rail. She grabbed onto a column and began climbing up.

"Here?" I asked. "I thought we'd fly around the yard."

"You know we need height to take off." She sounded like a teacher with a student who'd already forgotten yesterday's lesson.

"But the porch rail's a lot higher than the back of the couch." I glanced down to the yard. "I bet you're eight feet off the ground."

Polly just squinched her eyes shut. "I'm thinking about butterflies and blue jays," she said in a dreamy voice I was beginning to recognize. It sounded as if she were already in Neverland.

I hoped she was going to look before she took off. Just below the railing there was a wide thorny hedge that snaked its way around the porch. Landing on it would be like falling into the jaws of a snaggle-toothed crocodile.

But as if jumping weren't scary enough, Polly kept her eyes closed as she flung herself toward the yard. I felt as if I were holding her up with my gaze. She cleared the monster hedge and then kept going. It seemed like a long time before she hit the ground. I bit my lip as she rolled over twice and stopped, dead still.

When I looked up, Eileen was standing outside the fence with a hand over her mouth. Beside her, Timmy had a wide grin on his face.

"What are you two doing?" Eileen asked. But it sounded like she meant, "Are you two crazy?"

Polly's eyes snapped open. "We're learning to fly. Come on in—it's fun."

Timmy was off and running before Eileen could grab him.

I held tight to an ivy-covered column and climbed up on the railing. "Hey, Eileen!" I waved to her from the porch.

"You'd better watch out. That hedge is nothing but a giant pincushion," Eileen warned. "You're going to be holier than a priest if you land there."

"Not if I fly over it," I answered, trying to act as brave as Polly. I bent my knees and imagined birds in flight. I tried to close my eyes the way Polly had, but I just couldn't do it.

I took a deep breath, exhaled, and sprang. The instant I hit the air, I began screaming—high, sharp, and loud. To my ears, I sounded like an ambulance—which I hoped I wasn't going to need. I made it over the hedge by a couple of inches and came down hard, but standing. Then I staggered forward and collapsed in a heap.

"Lee, are you okay?" Eileen called.

"Sure, it was fun!" I answered. But she didn't hear me because Timmy had suddenly appeared on the porch rail.

"Timmy, get down from there!" she shrieked.

Timmy didn't answer. Or move. He stared straight ahead with his wide blue eyes and a poker-faced expression that reminded me of Jimmy Weenie. He bounced on the balls of his feet a few times as if he were testing a diving board.

"Don't jump too high, Tim! Don't jump too short! Don't close your eyes! Swing your arms forward!" Eileen kept babbling frantic instructions, but Timmy acted like he didn't hear a word. Without warning, he let go and leaped.

"Fly, Timmy, fly!" I found myself shouting.

Timmy's short legs jackknifed up toward his chest, and his arms pushed at the air. He just missed the hedge as he came down—all except for his shirt collar, which was snagged from behind on a thorn. Quickly, Eileen unhooked him and hugged him to her. That was when I saw the jagged red line on the back of his neck. Blood was trailing down into his shirt.

"Timmy!" Eileen cried.

Stuffed inside the pocket of my sweater was one of the hankies Mrs. Feldman had given me. I dabbed at Tim's neck with it while Eileen held him. With the blood wiped away, I could see it was only a scratch. But my heart was thumping against my chest like a ball being bounced off a wall. It could have been much worse.

Polly strolled over and placed a hand on Timmy's shoulder. She was smiling at him as if he were a real hero. Timmy's grimace turned into a grin. He squirmed away from Eileen and me.

"Let's have a sword fight!" Polly exclaimed. "There are some really good sticks in the backyard." She took off before she even finished her words.

Without hesitating for a second, Timmy ran after her. *"Tim!"* Eileen shouted, but she trailed right behind him.

I'd never thought about it before, but now I wondered if Eileen ever got tired of looking after her brother—and if he wished that she would let him alone sometimes. There seemed to be so many ways that a person could feel tied down. I guessed everyone had a reason for wanting to fly.

18

Your sword should be about the length of your arm," Polly said as if she were an expert.

I poked around the backyard until I found a stick that was pretty straight and about the width of a cat's tail. I wished I had a pocketknife so that I could peel off the bark, but my mother would never allow it.

"Get ready, here they come!" Polly announced, raising her stick above her head. She advanced toward a spot where sunlight shot through the trees in straight yellow rays like the ones in little kids' drawings. "Be gone or be sorry!" she called out.

Staring into the brightness made me squint. And when I did, I could almost make out something within the light. At first, it just looked like dust specks. But then I thought I could see the outline of a band of brawny pirates. Maybe it was a trick my eyes were playing. But just in case, I hoisted my stick. I noticed Eileen and Timmy did, too.

From behind us came a fluttering sound. We all turned around at once. Eileen actually squeaked. A flock of big blackbirds was settling into the twisty limbs of a huge, dark tree. Their eyes appeared to give off sparks of light.

"Talking blackbirds!" Polly whispered to us. "That's what the pirates of Neverland keep as pets instead of parrots. They're here to spy on us. We've got to chase them away!" With a cry of *Yah!* she began swinging her stick and running toward the tree.

I followed after her, shouting, "Shoo, scat!" as if they were cats. I didn't know what else to say to pirate birds. We surrounded the tree and began beating the trunk with our sticks.

Above us, the birds emitted low clicking noises I'd never heard before. It didn't sound like a call any bird from Brooklyn would have made. As if they had some magical signal, the flock flew off together like a dark cloud. Beneath the tree, we broke into cheers.

Polly brushed her hands together and beamed at us. "We've scared them away for now. But we'd all better stay on our guard. They'll be back, for sure."

I had a quick flash of fear, but it wasn't exactly unpleasant. It was more like the good-scary feeling of waiting in line to ride a really big roller coaster.

We stowed our swords under a bush. As I came out from behind the trellis, I glanced toward the street. Just outside the fence, Eddie Wagner was leaning against the maple tree, staring into the yard. I tried to ignore his smirk, but I could feel my face heating up. I wondered if he'd been listening to us.

"Who's that?" Polly asked.

"I have no idea," I answered, turning my back and heading for the porch. But Polly put a hand on my shoulder.

"Doesn't he look like a Lost Boy?" she whispered. "Look at his clothes."

I took another peek at Eddie. He had on the same blue jacket and pants he always wore. So what if the sleeves were too long and the pants were too short? I was sure Eddie didn't care what he looked like.

"Not to me he doesn't." I walked up the porch steps to retrieve my schoolbooks. I wasn't wasting another thought on Eddie Wagner.

When I looked down at the street again, he was gone. That was good. But when I turned back to the house, Mrs. Burke was staring at me through a parlor window. I hadn't realized she was home. I looked away quickly, pretending I hadn't seen her.

As I headed home along Avenue J, I slipped *George Washington Carver* out from my stack of books. Walking and reading at the same time was easy for me, although it seemed to surprise a lot of people. I wanted to finish the biography so I could start on my project. I wished I could be like George and discover something. When he was my age, he knew which roots in the woods would make laundry whiter and which leaves and flowers could make clothes smell sweet. But I didn't know of any woods in Brooklyn, and the only flowers that Zeke planted in front of our building were marigolds, which really reeked.

A weird clicking noise made me look up. At the corner, a blackbird sat atop a U.S. mailbox. The creature was as big as a cat. I couldn't help noticing its long, witchy toenails and flashing eyes.

I tiptoed a bit closer. When the bird didn't budge, I considered crossing the street. But I felt stupid. "Crows don't really spy, or talk, or attack people," I told myself. "That was just pretend." I hugged my books tighter and marched ahead.

The bird opened its beak and clicked at me. *Uck-uck-uck-issss! Uck-uck-uck-issss!*

"Nice birdy, nice birdy," I whispered.

It stretched its wings and puffed out its chest like a show-off—like those big cheesebrains, Gary and Larry. You couldn't let bullies know they were bothering you, or else they got more annoying. So I stamped my foot and shouted, "Fly away, birdbrain!"

Uck-uck-uck-issss! Uck-uck-uck-issss! This time the bird's warning seemed faster and angrier. Suddenly, it spread its wings and flew straight toward me. I drew back my arm and hurled *George Washington Carver* at it. Then I ducked, shrieking at the top of my lungs.

When I looked around again, it had disappeared.

My book was lying open on the sidewalk. As I picked it up, something fluttered out from between the pages—a small, white sheet of notepaper covered with tight, black handwriting. I reached out a foot and stepped on it.

Uck-uck-uck-issss! Uck-uck-uck-issss! I heard from behind me. I whirled around. Eddie Wagner was standing there, legs wide apart, arms flapping like a bird's wings.

"Ha-ha-ha!" He slapped his knee. "You thought I was one of those blackbirds! Ha-ha-ha!"

"Stop it!" I sputtered. "That wasn't funny!" I squeezed my eyes shut and bit my lip, but I couldn't stop tears from leaking down my cheeks.

"Stop it!" Eddie moaned, mimicking me. "It *was* funny. You were afraid of a bird."

"I wasn't!" I was surprised at how loud I'd screamed.

For a moment, Eddie looked startled, too. "Oh yeah? Then why are you crying?"

"I'm not. It's allergies. Some people are allergic to birds." As I rubbed my sleeve across my face, I centered my foot over the note so that only a corner stuck out. "What are you doing here, anyway? You're always sneaking around me like a stray cat. Don't you have a home to go to?"

Eddie's mouth twisted into a sneer. I could see his ugly chipped tooth, which was turning gray. "It's a free country, Snot-face," he snarled. He stepped off the curb and crossed the street. He didn't even look to see if there were any cars coming. In his faded blue jacket, his shoulders seemed more hunched than usual.

"Dogtooth!" I shot back as he skulked away. Polly was wrong—Eddie wasn't a Lost Boy, he was just a boy I wished would Get Lost. I wondered if he was as mean to his family as he was to everyone else. I'd never actually seen Eddie's mother or father—not even at the principal's office when he got in trouble. Maybe they didn't care about school, either.

I waited until Eddie was out of sight before

I grabbed the paper from under my shoe. Then I started running. I didn't stop until I got to my building. As soon as I squeezed into my hiding spot between the bushes, I felt safer. But I still couldn't stop my hands from shaking as I read the note.

The kingdom of heaven is like a large net that is cast in the sea, where it gathers all kinds of fish. When it is full, the fishermen pull it ashore and sort the fish. The good fish they put in baskets to take away, but the bad fish they throw away.

So it will be at the end of time. Angels will come and take away the good souls, but the evil ones will be thrown into the fiery furnace.
Matthew 13:47–49

Did Mrs. Burke mean me? Did she think I was a bad fish? "I'm not!" I murmured. But my heart began flapping as if it were trying to swim or fly. I was always arguing with Mom. Now I'd disobeyed about the bike. But Mrs. Burke couldn't have known about that, could she? She thought I was going to hell just because I was Jewish. That made me feel really sick— and worried. Because a tiny voice in my head was asking, *What if she was right?*

When I gazed around, it seemed as if all the houses,

trees, and telephone poles had grown taller—or that I'd gotten shorter. That was how I felt inside, too—small and weak. I looked up at the sky. It was still blue, but instead of bright and welcoming, it looked cold and empty. I clawed at the soil until I buried this note with the first. Then I fled upstairs.

After dinner, I curled up on the couch with my biography. Reading about George's life gave me so much to think about, it let me forget my own problems for a while. I was up to the part where George went to Washington, D.C. By now, he was so famous, Congress had asked him to explain why there should be a special tax to protect peanut farmers. He brought along evidence to support his case, just like Uncle Harold would. George's evidence included products he'd made from peanuts. But when he showed them the peanut milk he'd created, one congressman, John Tilson from Connecticut, asked, "Do you want a watermelon to go with that?"

It seemed like a weird question. I guess I looked confused because Dad asked, "Is something wrong, Lee?" He'd just come into the living room with his mystery book under his arm.

"I guess I don't understand politics." I showed him what Tilson said about the watermelon.

My father clamped his mouth shut. For a moment, I was afraid he was angry with me. But then he said, "That remark was Tilson's way of insulting Doctor Carver—and all Negroes—as slow, lazy folks who just want to sit around and eat watermelon."

"But John Tilson was a *congressman*, Dad."

"Yes—and he was also a bigot. Prejudice can happen anywhere. Here's the thing—few people today have any idea who Tilson was. But George Washington Carver is a national hero."

I knew Dad was trying to make me feel better. But what he'd said reminded me of Miss Hadley's words about things being unfair around here, too. It made my brain squirmy.

Dear Deb,

This will have to be my last letter, because I can't fit in writing with all the other stuff I have to do now. At school, Miss Hadley has given us a big biography project. My new friends practically beg me to come over every day after school. I hardly get a chance to do my homework anymore.

I have a boyfriend, too. He follows me everywhere. Sometimes he's a pain, but I know he can't help himself—he's a prisoner of passion. (Ha! Ha!) I guess you understand about boyfriends.

I bet you are having such a terrific time in Briny

Breezes, you hardly think about boring Brooklyn anymore. Maybe you haven't even had time to read my letters. Teena Weenie told me she wishes she could move to Florida, too. Are any houses for sale on your block? (Ha! Ha!)

Well, good-bye, Deb. In your ocean of friends, please think of me as a permanent wave.

Lee Bloom

19

When I heard Zeke humming, I let out my breath. I was glad I wouldn't be alone in the shadowy storage room. He was rolling an empty baby carriage back and forth to the tune of "Rock-a-Bye Baby." I let the door bang shut so he'd know he wasn't alone either.

Zeke stopped humming and looked up. "Going for a ride this morning?"

I opened my mouth to say yes, when something caught my eye. An orange tail waved from behind a tricycle. "Zeke, I think you've got a cat back there," I whispered.

"Yes, I do—an excellent mouse-catcher," Zeke said. "I have hired him to patrol the basement. He gets paid with Mary's leftovers."

I bent down and murmured, "Psst . . . psst . . .

psst." The cat threaded in and out of the bicycles right toward me. "I've seen this cat around before. I think its name is Reject."

Zeke shook his head. "I don't think that is the right name for him. Why don't you think of another?"

"Okay." I'd never had a chance to name a cat before. It purred happily when I petted its bony ribs. I was glad it was going to get to eat Mrs. Mayfield's cooking. "How about Lucky?"

"Lucky is a good name."

"Yeah." Reject made me think of the teenagers at the lunch counter in Miss Hadley's photograph. That's how they'd been treated—like rejects. It reminded me of something. "I might ride over to Woolworth's for lunch later," I said.

"This is Sunday. I believe they will be closed."

"Oh, right. I forgot." I watched Zeke turn the carriage tires one at a time. "Did you know you can get two hot dogs and an orange drink for a quarter at Woolworth's lunch counter?"

Zeke plucked a wrench and a can of 3-IN-1 oil from his toolbox. He didn't say anything. Maybe he didn't like hot dogs.

"But their orange drinks are awfully watery," I added as I wheeled the red bike to the door.

Zeke squirted some oil in the center of the left

front tire. "Mmmm," he mumbled. I wasn't sure if he was talking to the carriage or to me.

"Uh, the, um, tuna and pickle on toast is pretty good, though." I knew I was sounding dumber and dumber. I gave up and nosed my bike through the door.

"Yes, tuna is what I usually get," Zeke answered without looking up.

"You do? I'm really glad." I knew I sounded weird, but Zeke didn't seem to notice.

"Have a good ride," he called.

"Thanks, Zeke. See you later."

Before I got on my bike, I checked the sky. I wasn't sure what I was looking for—a plane shaped like a boat, or maybe a hot-air balloon full of sword-waving buccaneers. I wished I could visit Polly. I didn't exactly believe in invisible pirates, or Peter Pan, but I couldn't help thinking about the shadow I'd seen in the kitchen and the strange bird on the mailbox. When I was little, I used to make Dad check under my bed for alligators before I'd go to sleep. Naturally, I was too old to worry about alligators anymore. Still, a little part of me was asking why it was okay to believe in some invisible things like heaven and hell, and not in others like Neverland.

But today was Sunday, and Mrs. Burke would

probably be home, so I headed for the park. I was beginning to love how free biking made me feel. Since I could already walk and read, I decided to try pedaling and reading. The problem was, I lost my place every time I bounced over a crack or bump.

The swings at the park were toddler-sized, but there were benches to sit on. I figured I could finish *George Washington Carver* if I concentrated for a while. At the start of the last chapter, there was a portrait of George that a famous artist had made three months before George died. He was in a crisp white apron, examining a big, beautiful flower that my book said was an amaryllis. I studied his proud, happy smile, and I smiled, too—until something bumped the bench I was sitting on. A bicycle tire. I looked up.

Eddie Wagner was smirking over the handlebars. "What are you doing here, Skippy? Did a bird chase you?" he jeered.

"It's a free country, remember? I can go anywhere I want." I looked down at my book.

"You still reading that? I finished *Luther Burbank* a week ago."

"Right. And I guess you did your project, too," I said, without taking my eyes off the page.

"I started it. It needs time to take off."

I knew I should ignore him, but I couldn't. "You

expect me to believe that? You don't even do the regular homework."

"So?" Eddie brought his face right down to mine.

"So I think you're lying." I would've called him Dogtooth, but he looked like he was ready to choke me.

I shifted my gaze to his bike—a pearly blue racer with narrow tires—and something clicked in my brain. "Hey, I know this bike!" I burst out. "You stole it from our basement storage room!"

Eddie got off his bike and raised a fist. It was too late to run, so I gritted my teeth, shut my eyes, and waited to be slugged. Instead, I heard a *clang!* as he kicked my parked bike. It fell over onto the dirt like a dead thing. The handlebar struck my anklebone.

"Ow, hey, stop!" I shouted. "That bike's not even mine, you, you . . . thief!" But Eddie kicked the bicycle again—harder this time. I jumped up from the bench and tried to grab his handlebars. But faster than you could say "bullcrud," he sped away.

Mom was fussing with some little green shoots when I came home. She was always trying to grow new plants from cuttings or seeds. I wished she could have a real, outdoor garden instead of a bunch of windowsills for her plants. I thought she might be happy in a garden.

"Did you have a nice walk?" she asked.

"Mmmph," I mumbled. I picked up her watering can so I wouldn't have to look her in the eye. "Want me to give the plants a drink?"

"Sure. Feel them first to see who's dry."

All of a sudden, I made a decision. "Mom, I want to grow peanuts for my biography project," I said.

"Peanuts? I'm not sure you can get peanuts from plants grown indoors. It's tricky."

I reached out and fiddled with her apron strings. "I'd like to try, though."

Mom nodded. "Well, you'll need raw peanuts. All we have is a jar of the roasted, salted kind. I think you can get raw ones at the greengrocer's. Better go tomorrow, after school. It's going to take a while for them to grow."

"How long?"

"For the plants, a few weeks. For the peanuts—months."

"Months?" It looked like even Dogtooth was going to have a finished project before me. I could already imagine him gloating about it.

"Can you answer that?" Mom waved her dirt-spattered fingers toward the phone.

"Lee, you've got to come over!" Polly whispered when I said hello.

"Now?"

"*Something's happened.*" She was speaking really quickly. "The pirates are trapped in the attic. Peter glued the windows and door shut with crocodile spit. But I can hear them trying to get out. We have to launch an attack right away."

The pirates were in her attic? I felt as if a dumbwaiter were dropping inside me. I stretched out the phone cord and squeezed into the coat closet.

"Is your mother home?"

"Yes, why?"

I leaned my cheek against Mom's blue wool coat. "No reason. I was just curious." For a second, I let myself wonder if she knew about her mother's notes. I was sure she didn't. But what if I told her? I knew how Polly would feel then—the same way I would feel if she heard the things my mom said about people who weren't Jewish. My face got hot just thinking about it.

"I've got to finish a book for school. I can't come today," I said. It was true, although I'd decided I would try to visit only when Mrs. Burke wasn't around. On the other end of the line, I heard Polly's breathing get quicker, as if she were really frightened. The dumbwaiter inside me dropped again.

"I don't know how much longer that croc spit will hold them," Polly said. "Can you come after school tomorrow?"

"I have to run an errand first. But I could stop by afterward for a little while."

"Okay. Come as fast as you can."

The closet door creaked open a bit. "Aaah!" I squealed.

Mikey laughed and crawled in with me. "Peek-a-buh!" he crowed.

"I've got to go now," I told Polly.

"Lee, wait. Keep your windows closed tonight in case they escape," she warned.

20

Pirates in Brooklyn! What would Deb have said if I'd told her? Probably she would have laughed or called it a baby game. But there was no sense wondering what Deb thought anymore, I reminded myself. Besides, it *was* only pretend. Even so, I felt prickles of excitement up and down my back. I couldn't wait until tomorrow.

In the middle of the night, I awoke to a scratching at the window. When I opened my eyes, a long, bony finger was feeling the pane. *Scritch. Scritch. Scriiiitch.*

I held my breath. The window was closed, but I wasn't sure it was locked. I slipped out of bed and crept across the room. The finger—and whomever it belonged to—was gone. Then I remembered that, except for their shadows, Peter and the pirates were invisible. Maybe one was looking at me right now.

With a trembling hand, I checked the lock. It was latched tight. Mikey and I were safe.

I ran back to bed and pulled up the covers. Then I glanced across the room to make sure I hadn't woken the baby. Mikey's crib was empty.

Outside my room, something creaked. My heart was jumping all over my chest as I held my breath and tiptoed to the door. A shadowy figure with a bundle on its shoulder was heading down the hall. The bundle squirmed and whimpered—it was my brother.

"Mom! Dad! Come quick!" I screamed. "A pirate is stealing the baby!"

Mikey began wailing. The shadowy figure whirled around toward me, pointing its bony finger.

"Lee, shhh! You're having a nightmare, honey." Mom patted Mikey on his back to calm him. "Your brother's got a little fever."

"But I saw something at the window," I blurted out. "It was trying to get us." Suddenly I was confused and exhausted.

"Go back to bed now," my mother whispered as the baby dozed on her shoulder. "It's all right. We're safe here."

All day I was tired in school. Afterward, I practically dragged myself to the greengrocer's. But I perked up when I found a bin heaped with raw peanuts. I bought a small brown bag and tucked it under my arm.

On the way home, I stopped at Polly's. I hadn't forgotten the long, gnarled finger I thought I'd seen at the windowpane. It was just pretend, but I wanted to check that the pirates were still trapped in the attic. Polly was out on the porch. When she saw me, she came running down the steps. "Look!" She pointed at the sky. "That's their flying galleon. They've disguised it as a cloud."

I looked up and saw a huge, boat-shaped cloud floating over Avenue J. It was curved at the bottom, with three puffs like billowy sails at the top.

"They're planning to take us back to Neverland in it," Polly whispered. "We have to help Peter defeat them once and for all."

"Are they still in the attic?" I asked. "I thought one was trying to get in through my window last night."

Polly nodded. "It was probably Smee. Peter didn't catch him with the others because he stayed behind to mind the pirate ship."

Scriiitch. Suddenly I heard a creak. Polly and I both jumped.

"Polly, come in and brush your teeth. It's almost time to go." Mrs. Burke was leaning out of a second-floor window. "Hello, Lee," she added, barely glancing at me. She pulled back in before I found my tongue.

Polly turned back to me and shrugged her shoulders. "Dentist appointment today."

"But what about the pirates?" My heart was still bouncing like a runaway ball. "What if they break out?"

"Don't worry. Peter ran extra crocodile spit around the door last night. I did the windows myself. It should hold them until tomorrow. I'll ask Eileen and Timmy to come help us fight."

"They know?" I'd thought I was the only one Polly had trusted with the secret.

"Sort of. They think it's just a game." Polly reached into the pocket of her jacket and pulled out a bright green feather. "Here, take this for protection tonight. Just in case."

"It's pretty, but where—"

"It's from one of Peter's magic parrots."

"I thought they had blackbirds."

"Those are the pirates' birds. Peter and his Lost Boys have beautiful green parrots." Polly stroked the feather lightly. Then she placed it in my palm. "It's good for one wish. But don't use it unless you absolutely have to." She peered up at the house once more and ran inside.

21

The moment I saw Mom, I could tell something was wrong. Her face was scrunched the way it got when she had a headache, and her eyes were darker than the black coffee she was drinking. I wondered if she'd found out about the borrowed bike.

"Hi, Mom. I have so much homework today. I'd better go start it." I hurried to my room and put my books and the bag of peanuts on my bed. The feather I shoved under my pillow.

"Lee? I want to talk to you about something."

I turned around. Mom was standing in the doorway. "Okay." I plopped my backside down on the pillow.

My mother came and sat beside me. "Aunt Bea is in the hospital."

I felt my throat tighten. "Why? What's wrong with her?"

"Her heart isn't working properly." A strand of hair was hanging in Mom's eyes. I wanted to brush it away, but something about my mother was saying, "Don't touch."

I knew Aunt Bea had had rheumatic fever as a girl. It left her heart weak the way polio had left Deb with weak legs. Mom told me it was the reason my aunt and uncle couldn't have any children.

My whole chest felt wound up so tight I could barely breathe. "Is she going to get better?"

Mom picked at her skirt with her long fingers. I wasn't sure she was going to answer. "They're giving her medicine now, and they may try to do a procedure."

I had to clear my throat before I could ask, "You mean operate?"

"Yes." Mom reached over and took my hand. Hers was so cold that I flinched inside. But I sat very still while she braided her fingers through mine.

Aunt Bea was the one who held our family together. She was kind and wise. I loved her so much.

I guess I noticed the sloshing sound before Mom. "Did you leave the water running in the kitchen?" I asked.

"I don't think so." We jumped up and followed the sound to the kitchen.

Water was dripping from the windowsill, the table, the floor, and my brother. "I wawder!" Mikey announced, waving the empty watering can.

Mom gazed at the sopping wet kitchen and my sopping wet brother.

"You did a very thorough job, Mikey," I said. "Come on, I'll change you." I hoisted him up and carried him into our bedroom.

After I changed his diaper, I dug in his drawer and found him a new shirt, some blue corduroy overalls, and a pair of socks that I didn't recognize. They were parrot green and large enough to fit someone my age.

I took a sniff, but the socks only smelled like Spin, our usual laundry detergent.

"Look at these, Mikey—big, green socks," I said, waving them around.

My brother wriggled his tiny toes. "Zhreen, zhreen!"

"But they're much too big for you."

"Zhreen, zhreen!"

I tickled the soles of his feet. "Mikey, do you know how these socks got in the bureau?"

My brother only laughed. I reached back into the drawer and found a little red pair. "Now your feet are red like a fire engine," I said as I wrestled them on him.

But as he toddled away, Mikey chanted, "Zhreen, zhreen, zhreen, zhreen!"

My mother was pushing a mop back and forth over the kitchen floor. It was only spreading the water around more, but she didn't seem to notice.

"Mom, whose are these?" I asked, dangling the strange socks.

"I don't know." She didn't even glance at them.

"They were in Mikey's drawer. Look—they're way too big for him."

"They must be a pair you outgrew. You've probably just forgotten about them."

I had to fight not to raise my voice. "I wouldn't have forgotten these. They're weird."

My mother kept on mopping, but she was looking out the window. "Maybe they're your father's."

"They're green, Mom." She knew perfectly well that my father only wore black socks or brown ones. He didn't own any others.

"Just put them in Dad's drawer, Lee."

Suddenly, I was shouting. *"Look at them, Mom!* Dad wouldn't wear these socks in a million years. They're bright green!" Before I could think about it, I jerked back my arm and let them fly from my fingers like a baseball—right at my mother.

Thwack! The socks smacked her chest and fell to the

wet floor. But she just picked them up and laid them on the table.

"Mom, I'm sorry—" I began.

"They must have gotten mixed up with our clothes in the laundry room. Put them in the basket, and I'll return them the next time I go down there." There wasn't one drop of anger in her voice. That hurt worse than anything.

I took the socks and slunk out. But instead of tossing them in the basket, I brought them back to my room. From under my pillow, I removed the feather Polly had given me. The color matched the socks exactly.

A weird feeling crept over me. *What if they were Peter Pan's socks?* What if he'd left them in my room as a sign that he'd truly been here the night I'd seen his shadow? I touched the place on my ear where I'd felt the brush of a feather. I closed my eyes and saw the point of his hat and his long, slim legs on the wall.

If Peter Pan was real, then anything could be possible—blackbirds that spied on people . . . a band of invisible pirates . . . Mrs. Burke's burning-hot hell.

"Please don't let Aunt Bea die," I whispered. "She's a good person. Mom needs her—we all do." I wasn't sure if it counted as a prayer, but I hoped God could hear me.

I glanced at the doorway before I shoved the socks under my pillow. But I held the feather in my palm awhile, wondering if I should make a wish. I decided it would be better to wait and see what happened, so I slipped the feather under the pillow again. It was silly, but I felt better knowing it was there.

22

The next morning, my pajamas were damp with sweat, and I felt as if I'd stayed up much too late. I staggered to the bathroom and peered into the mirror over the sink. Beneath my eyes were blue-black shadows that curved like wings. My curls were wild and tangled like the vines in a fairy-tale forest. I liked the way they made me appear brave and even a little tough—like a girl a pirate might think twice about trying to kidnap. I decided not to comb them.

"Be sure to come straight home after school," Mom said when I entered the kitchen. She didn't mention my hair.

I felt my heart drop. "Why? Is Aunt Bea worse?"

"I won't know anything until Uncle Harold phones from the hospital. I need to stay here and wait for the call. We're out of juice and cold cuts, and lots of other things, so you'll have to do the shopping today."

I was really worried about Aunt Bea, but I was a little disappointed, too. I'd been planning to fight pirates this afternoon. Instead, I was going to buy bologna.

"Okay," I agreed. "But why don't you go to the hospital?"

"Aunt Bea is too sick for visitors. Uncle Harold is the only one allowed."

Seeing Mom's eyes well up brought a fat lump to my throat. "I'm not hungry," I croaked. "I'll just go to school."

Mom never let me go anywhere without breakfast. But she didn't say a word as I got my sweater out of the closet and headed for the door.

I had one foot in the hallway when I remembered the socks and the feather, so I tiptoed back to my room and pulled them from under my pillow. Then I stuffed them into my sweater pockets. Mikey was still in his crib, sucking his morning bottle with a soft *shoosh . . . shoosh . . . shoosh* sound. I leaned over the rail and kissed him on the forehead. "I'll see you later," I whispered. "Don't go anywhere with strangers, okay?"

The first thing I noticed when I tried to slide my books into my desk was a wad of crumpled papers. I didn't remember leaving any garbage in there. I tried to keep the papers from rustling as I pulled the wad out and smoothed it flat on my desktop. When I real-ized what it was, I let out a little yelp. Mrs. Burke's notes! How could they have gotten into my desk?

All of my classmates were staring at me. So was Miss Hadley. "Lee, is something wrong?" she asked.

"I think I may have gotten a splinter from inside my desk," I said, staring at my thumb. With my other hand, I slipped a book over the notes.

Miss Hadley started up the aisle. "Do you want me to take a look?"

I held my thumb closer to my face. "No, I guess I just pricked it."

Across the aisle, Eddie was scratching something into his desktop. When I realized what he was writ-ing, I almost yelped again. He was writing HELL in capital letters.

That made me realize something. Eddie was the only one who knew about my spot between the hedges. He must have dug up the notes and put them in my desk.

I leaned across the aisle. "Rat! Freak! Moron!"

"Heh-heh," Eddie sniggered, low enough so the teacher couldn't hear.

"Lee?" Miss Hadley said.

I lowered my voice and whispered, "Go to hell, Dogtooth!"

"Lee, is something wrong?"

Everything was wrong. But I could only shake my head no.

"Then please take out your reader and do the assignment on the board like the rest of your classmates. *Right now!*"

I pulled out my book and slammed it onto my desktop. I didn't care who was watching. Why didn't Miss Hadley tell Eddie to take out his reader? I couldn't believe I'd ever thought she was nice.

At three o'clock, I stuffed Mrs. Burke's notes into my pocket and ran home as fast as I could. Mom looked really tired when she opened the door.

"Did you hear from Uncle Harold?" I asked.

"A little while ago," she whispered, as if the baby were napping, though he was right under the table pushing Gooey in his dump truck.

"How is Aunt Bea?"

"They had to drain some fluid from around her heart. Uncle Harold says she's resting comfortably."

"That's good, isn't it?"

Mom nodded. But a tear rolled down her cheek.

"Don't cry, Mom. She'll get better now." I put my arms around her and rubbed her back. But I felt scared. I wanted Mom to be the brave one.

I stepped back and smoothed out my sweater. "Do you have a grocery list?"

"Here." From her apron pocket she pulled out a sheet of paper and some money. "You can pick up the cart downstairs. One of the wheels was sticking, so I left it with Zeke."

I scanned the list. There were a lot of items, but I thought if I hurried, I still might be able to go to Polly's after I'd dropped Mom's stuff at home.

Zeke wasn't in the lobby. I knocked at his apartment door. No one answered, so I headed outside. Gary and Larry were in front of the building, tossing a ball.

"Has either of you seen Zeke?" I asked. The ball whizzed by my nose.

"Yeah, Wormhead, I saw him," Gary said.

"Are you gonna tell me where, Cheesebrain?" The ball breezed past my cheek as Larry chucked it back.

"He's in the alley with your favorite juvenile delinquent—Eddie."

"With Eddie?"

"Yeah, don't you know he's Zeke's assistant now? I thought Eddie was your boyfriend, Wormhead."

I turned and started running. The ball bounced off my back, but I kept going.

In the alley behind our building, Zeke and Eddie

were crouched next to the pearly blue bike. Lucky was rubbing up against Eddie's knee.

"Hold this chain while I wind it tight. Watch your fingers, son," Zeke said. He looked up and saw me before I could leave. "Hello, Lee. Do you know Ed?"

Eddie gave a teeny nod.

"Um, Mom's shopping cart," I blurted out.

"It's all ready. Ed and I just fixed it." Zeke turned to Eddie. "Would you please bring out the cart?"

Eddie jumped up and headed through the door to the basement. In school, Miss Hadley practically had to beg him to do anything at all.

I began stroking Lucky so I wouldn't have to look at Zeke. I couldn't believe how nicely he was treating *Ed*—like he was someone special. I'd always believed Zeke thought I was special. But it looked like he'd given Eddie the racing bike. I'd only gotten the dumpy red one.

I wished I could tell Zeke how Eddie had dug up those notes and put them in my desk—how he'd even laughed about it. If I did, I was sure Zeke wouldn't be so friendly to him. But I remembered what Uncle Harold said about proof. Since I didn't have any, I kept quiet.

Eddie came up the basement ramp pulling the cart

behind him. He parked it in front of me without looking at me.

"Ed took the nut off the bad wheel and cleaned the rust from underneath it," Zeke said. "He oiled all four of them for you."

"Thanks," I mumbled. Carefully, I wrapped my fingers around the handle, trying to avoid the places Eddie had touched.

At the grocery store, I couldn't stop thinking about Zeke and Eddie. I couldn't believe Zeke had been fooled into thinking *Ed* was a good kid. I kept clearing my throat to get rid of the lump of anger that was stuck there. But the more I thought, the bigger that lump grew.

"Anything wrong, dear?" The woman in front of me looked concerned.

"Just allergies," I choked.

She dug in her purse and offered me a cherry-menthol cough drop. The smell made me think of Eddie. I was afraid it might make me throw up, but the lady was watching me.

"Thank you," I said, sliding it onto my tongue. I was grateful when the cashier asked her how she wanted her coffee ground. As soon as the woman turned back around, I spit the cough drop into the flowered hankie. Silently, I thanked Mrs. Feldman. I was beginning to understand how valuable a handkerchief could be.

I checked Mom's list as I put the items on the conveyer belt. Everything was there, plus one thing she hadn't asked for—a black-and-gold container with a picture of a tall-masted sailboat on the front. I picked it up and read the label.

PIRATE'S BOOTY TALCUM
"Turns pirates into gentlemen"

I gasped so loudly, both the cashier and the woman turned to stare.

I tried to think how or when that powder had gotten in with my groceries. Had it fallen into the cart when I'd reached for a can of shaving cream for Dad? Had I knocked it in when I picked up a container of Mikey's baby powder? Or had an invisible hand placed it there to help me?

I still had time to run back to the toiletries aisle and return it. But I put the Pirate's Booty on the counter with my other things. I had enough allowance to pay for it myself. Just maybe, I'd need it later.

23

It was hard to run to Polly's. The can of pirate powder kept banging against my hip. I was getting so sore, I gave up and walked the rest of the way. I hoped I hadn't missed the entire battle.

But when I got to the house, the yard was empty. So was the porch. I looked up at the half-moon windows. They were dark and blank. Even the air seemed more still than was normal.

I ran up the steps and pressed the doorbell. No one came. I rang again and waited, but my insides were sinking. What if the pirates had won? What if they had taken Polly, Eileen, and Timmy with them? I looked up for the cloud-shaped ship. It was gone.

Suddenly, the door flew open. Polly adjusted her glasses on her nose as if she were surprised. "Hi, Lee. I didn't think you were coming."

"Where are Eileen and Timmy?"

"Gone."

"But—" I looked up at the sky.

"Oh, no." Polly giggled. "They could only stay for a little while. They had to go home and clean their rooms."

"What happened? Did you have the battle?"

"The battle?" Polly wrinkled her forehead. "Oh! Didn't you see Peter? I asked him to fly over yesterday and tell you."

From inside one of my pockets, I felt a strange throb. When I reached in, my hand brushed Mrs. Burke's notes. I pushed them down farther and pulled out the green socks. "I didn't exactly see him. But I found these in my brother's drawer yesterday."

Polly grabbed her glasses as if she couldn't believe her eyes. "Peter's socks! He must have left them for you. I bet you weren't home when he flew over to tell you that the pirates got out an attic window. The croc spit dissolved, and we didn't have any more. They flew away in their ship." She pointed toward the sky. "See? It's gone."

I looked up and saw nothing but boring blue. "Yeah. I guess we can stop worrying about them." I tried not to sound disappointed.

"Are you kidding?" Polly's voice got really high.

"Now it's going to be even worse. They'll be bringing reinforcements back. Whole swarms of pirates! Peter flew back to Neverland to ask the Lost Boys to help us."

"Well, he's going to have cold feet when he gets there," I said, tossing the socks up and catching them in one hand.

Polly didn't laugh as she reached out a finger and touched them. "I bet they have magic powers." She swung the door open wider. "Come on in. We'd better keep practicing our flying so we'll be ready when Peter comes back."

I looked past her into the house, listening for sounds. I didn't hear anything. Or anyone.

"My mother won't be home for an hour. She's working in Dad's office today," Polly said. She'd read my mind, but it wasn't spooky. I kind of liked it.

I ran up the staircase after her. At the top of the first landing, I stopped to examine something that hadn't been there before. On the little table against the wall, someone had set out a framed photograph surrounded by miniature American flags. There was also a goblet filled with a golden liquid sitting on a lacy white doily.

"Was your dad in the army?" I asked, gazing at the photo of a skinny young man in a soldier's uniform.

Polly came back down from the next staircase. "Oh, that's not my father. It's Uncle Frank, my mom's younger brother. Today's his birthday."

"Does he live far away?"

She lowered her eyelids. "He was killed in the war. He was eighteen."

"I guess your mother misses him a lot."

"She says he's our guardian angel in heaven now." Polly ran a finger along the top of the frame. "I wish I could have met him."

"My grandparents died in the war, too," I said.

"Then they're your guardian angels."

I didn't answer. The only angels I'd ever seen were on Christmas cards. They were all slender with blue eyes and flowing blonde hair. On her dresser, Aunt Bea had a photograph of my grandparents. Their hair and eyes were dark, and they looked quite plump. They weren't exactly smiling, but their faces seemed peaceful and content, the way I imagined an angel's would.

Once, when I'd asked Dad what happened to people after they died, he'd said they lived on in our hearts. I liked the idea of carrying a little bit of my grandparents inside me. Maybe it was like having guardian angels—only in a different way.

I pointed to the goblet. "What's in here?"

"Champagne. Mom always pours Uncle Frank a glass to celebrate his birthday." Silently, she gazed at the ceiling. But when she looked back down, there was a grin on her face. "You know, I think Uncle Frank is thirsty. He hasn't had a drink in a long time." She picked up the glass, took a sip, and held it out to me.

I'd never had champagne before, but at Passover, Uncle Harold always poured me a taste of sweet grape wine. It brought tears to my eyes, but I pretended to like it anyway. I took the goblet from Polly and gulped a mouthful. The champagne tasted so tart, it made my tongue shrink back and my eyes moisten. It burned all the way down my throat and into my stomach and made me speechless. While I waited for the feeling to ease up, I gazed at the picture of Mrs. Burke's younger brother. He looked friendly and nice—and hardly older than a kid.

I couldn't imagine anything more awful than losing Mikey. It looked like Mrs. Burke had felt that way about her brother, too. It made me think of something Aunt Bea had told me about my own mother. She'd said Mom's bad moods weren't my fault, but that they were because of a hurt deep inside her. I wondered if Polly's mother's hurt had made her moody.

Polly and I traded the glass back and forth until

it was empty. "Won't Mom be surprised!" she exclaimed as she put it back on the doily.

"Do you think she'll really believe Frank drank it?" I asked.

Polly shrugged. "Maybe. My mother is a woman of strong beliefs." Suddenly, she whirled away toward the staircase. "Come on. Let's practice flying."

Without talking about it, we set up the island of cushions farther away from the couch than usual. I guessed I could read Polly's mind, too. "You go first," she said. She crossed the room and leaned against the far wall to watch.

"Okay." I pulled the green socks out of my pocket. "You think I ought to put these on?"

"Definitely."

I pulled them over my own white socks. Right away, something seemed different. I climbed up on the back of the sofa. A funny, buzzy sensation was making my body tingle as if a power switch inside me had been turned on. I stood with my toes curled over the edge and thought about the way seagulls at the beach hovered without flapping their wings. My arms stretched and curved. A breeze ruffled over them.

And I was flying.

Suddenly I was up near the ceiling, floating gently

and easily. I looked down at the island of cushions and studied the little nicks and creases in the leather. I counted the floorboards across the room. I felt quivery and weightless up there. I thought that if the windows were open, I might drift away.

I guess I was holding my breath, because suddenly I had to suck in a lot of air. It made me hiccup—and I came crashing down in the middle of the cushions.

For a moment, I was too stunned to move. And then I began shrieking. "Did you see? Did you see? I flew!"

"Yes, yes!" Polly flopped down beside me. "Peter's socks must have worked. I can't wait to tell him."

"Here, now you put them on." I slipped off the socks and held them out.

Polly flopped back on the cushions. "I don't think I could fly now. I'm really tired. You do it again and I'll watch."

I wasn't feeling so great myself. Besides, although being able to fly felt amazing, it was also a little scary. "I can't either. My stomach's queasy. I think I'm seasick—or airsick."

"Okay, let's wait till later."

We lolled around on the cushions, not saying much. I guess we were both in shock. But after a while, a question popped into my head. "Where do you think Neverland is?"

Polly propped herself up on an elbow. "I don't know. Somewhere in the sky or in outer space."

"Isn't that where heaven is?"

"Probably."

"What about hell?"

"I don't know. Why?"

I sat up and hugged my knees. "I was just thinking about the rules."

"What rules?"

"About who gets to go where. Your uncle Frank's in heaven, Peter and the pirates are in Neverland"—I gazed out the window—"and Jews go to hell."

"I don't believe that Jews go to hell, Lee."

"Some people do," I said softly.

"But I don't! It wouldn't be fair, otherwise. And God has to be fairer than people are. That's why He's God."

I reached for one of her wispy braids and took the rubber band off the end. Careful not to tug, I began rebraiding it more neatly. "Do you think Jews go to heaven?"

"Definitely. I wouldn't want to go there if they didn't."

I shot her a sideways glance. "You'd rather go to hell?"

"No, just somewhere different. A place we could go together." Suddenly her face lit up. "Like Neverland."

It was such a crazy, funny idea that I couldn't help laughing. But the strange thing was, I felt more like crying. How could such a fair person have such an unfair mother?

After I finished her other braid, Polly looked at her watch. "My mom will be home soon."

I nodded. For the first time, I thought she might know about her mother's notes, after all . . . only now it didn't matter. I stood up and walked slowly toward the door. Flying had left my legs and my stomach feeling a little woozy.

"I'll call you as soon as the pirates come back," Polly promised. "Be ready!"

24

On the way home, my head was spinning, and all I wanted to do was lie down. At first I thought it was from flying, but now it felt more like I was coming down with something.

"Hello there, Lee," a voice said as I staggered toward the front of the building.

I noticed the sticks and twigs on the ground first. Then I peeked behind the hedges and found Zeke with his clippers.

"Hi, Zeke."

"How is your aunt Bea? Your father mentioned that she was in the hospital."

"We don't know yet." I started for the door.

"I see." Zeke pushed back his cap. "How was the shopping cart?"

"It was okay." I already had the door open, but Zeke didn't seem to notice.

"I thought Ed would do a good job. That's why I lent him that blue racing bike we had in the storage room. It needed some work, and I knew he liked fixing things. Who knows? Maybe someday he will actually be a mechanic."

"Or a criminal," I mumbled without turning around. I was sick of Eddie. I hated knowing that he'd borrowed a bike, too. I didn't want to be in any category that he was a part of.

"Pardon?" Zeke said as if he hadn't heard me.

"Nothing." I slipped my hand into my sweater pocket and fingered the crumpled notes.

"It is a shame Ed has no friends around here. With his parents both gone, he must be pretty lonesome. I know his grandfather tries, but that boy is on his own a lot." Zeke began gathering up the twigs he'd cut. "Being lonely can make a person feel worthless. It can make someone act in a way—"

Suddenly I was shouting. "Why are you telling me? I don't care about Eddie! You don't know anything about it, anyway! You're not his father, you're just a super!"

For an instant, I was so shocked at myself, I couldn't move. I just kept staring at Zeke. His face seemed to grow longer, and his nostrils were twitching with an angry expression I'd never seen on him. Then I was inside the apartment building, pounding up the stairs. Angry tears were spilling down my face.

Mom was sitting at the table when I came in, but I rushed straight to the bathroom without saying anything to her. I turned on the water while I sobbed into a towel. When I was finally able to stop, I washed my face in cold water and waited for my breathing to return to normal. In the mirror, I looked at my red-rimmed eyes and hoped Mom wouldn't notice.

But she was fixing a button on one of Dad's shirts and didn't even look up when I came into the kitchen. Under the table, Mikey was quietly gnawing a bagel. I pulled off my sweater, dropped it on a chair, and got down to join him there.

I cleared my throat. "Did you hear from Uncle Harold again?"

"Yes. He said Bea was awake for a little while. She told him he'd better not be eating jelly donuts for dinner while she was away."

"She made a joke? She must be feeling a little better." I imagined the corners of my aunt's mouth twitching upward as she scolded my uncle.

Mom didn't answer.

"Do you think I could plant those raw peanuts

now, Mom?" I was trying to ignore the queasiness in my stomach, but it was hard to sound normal.

"I suppose so."

I went to the cabinet for a pie pan and the potting soil.

"Oh, you won't need soil yet," Mom said.

"Why not?"

"The best way to sprout peanuts is to start them between wet paper towels. They need to be kept moist and warm. After the seedlings appear, you can plant them."

"How'd you know that?"

"I must have read it somewhere."

"George Washington Carver would have been proud of you," I said, but it was hard to tell if she'd heard me.

I laid a wet paper towel in the pie pan, put the peanuts on it, and covered the whole thing with plastic wrap. In spite of everything that had happened, I felt a little better as I set it on the windowsill. I could understand why my mother liked gardening so much. Thinking about growing something new was exciting. It was kind of like having a toe in the future.

"Lee, are you all right? You look so pale," Mom said as if she'd finally noticed me.

"Maybe I am a little tired," I told her. "I'll just lie down for a while."

I was stretched out on my bed with my eyes closed, but I wasn't sleeping. I was wishing I could talk to Aunt Bea. Sometimes it seemed like words flew out of my mouth before I could stop them. That's what happened with Zeke. *You're just a super!* How could I have said that to him? I'd sounded like the people who'd called George Washington Carver "Washwoman." Like people who thought they were too good to eat with Negroes.

My father had said that prejudice could be anywhere. But I'd never thought it could be inside me. It made me feel hateful. With all my heart, I knew I didn't want to be that kind of person. Only, Zeke would never believe that now. I remembered how shocked and angry his face had looked, and I wished I could crawl out of my skin. Maybe I did deserve to go to hell.

I opened my eyes. Mom was standing over me, holding a wad of crumpled paper. "These notes fell out of your sweater while I was hanging it in the closet."

I felt a band of fear tightening around my stomach. "Did you read them?"

She nodded.

I sat up. "It's just a bunch of stupid stuff. We should ignore it, right?"

"No, Lee, we shouldn't." I was surprised at how loud and sharp Mom's voice was. She dropped the notes onto my lap. "Who gave you these?"

I stared at my mother, too afraid to speak.

"I asked who gave you these—answer me!"

I looked down at my hands. "Eddie Wagner." I told myself it was partly the truth. But another part of my mind was shocked at my lie. The strange thing was, Mom looked surprised, too.

"Do you know him?" I asked.

"A little. I met him in the basement while I was doing laundry." She turned the notes over on their backs. "I'm glad to see Eddie doesn't agree with this."

"What do you mean?"

"Didn't you see what he wrote here?" Mom held one of the notes under my nose. Scribbled in pencil were the words, *This is bullcrud!*

"Lee, I want you to tell me who gave you these papers. *Now!*"

"Mrs. Burke," I whispered.

Mom hugged her middle as if she were trying to keep herself from flying apart. "From now on, I want you to stay away from that woman. And her daughter, too."

"No, Mom, wait!" I jumped up and grabbed her arm. "You don't understand. Polly didn't have anything to do with it. She doesn't believe that stuff. Really."

"No, Lee, *you* don't understand. You're too young to realize what words like these can do. They twist minds. They turn people into beasts who do terrible things."

I tried to sound reasonable. "I won't go over there. I'll meet Polly at the park or invite her to come here. That way you can see she's not like her mother."

"Absolutely not. I don't want that girl anywhere near here."

"That's not fair! You don't know her—"

"I don't need to. You think people like the Burkes care what you're like?"

"People like the Burkes! People like the Burkes!" I shouted. "You're as bad as they are. You call people *goyim* and *schwartzers*. You say the Burkes eat horses and pigeons. You won't let Zeke give me a bike because you think we're too good to take gifts from Negroes. You're no different than Mrs. Burke! And now you're trying to make me that way!"

"You don't know what you're saying!" My mother's voice was becoming raspy from shouting. "You're only a child! You have no idea what the world is really like! When you get older, you'll understand that it's better to stick with your own kind. You can never really trust anyone else." Mom dismissed me with a wave of her hand and turned to leave.

"But we're hardly Jewish anyway!" I screamed at her back.

She spun around with a raised arm.

"How dare you? My own parents died trying to make sure that I could live without having to fear who I was—*a Jew!*"

I waited for the slap, but she dropped her arm as if I wasn't worth the effort. For a moment I couldn't feel, or see, or hear anything—except for the ringing in my ears. That's when I realized that Mikey was in the doorway, wailing. But Mom brushed right by him as she stalked out. In another moment, the front door slammed.

"Shh, Mikey, it's okay." I lifted my brother into my arms and patted him on the back. When he quieted down, he laid his head on my shoulder and twisted his fingers through my hair. Each little tug felt precious.

25

Outside the window, the moon looked like a picture in a baby's book—a glowing yellow banana on a smooth black tablecloth. I stared at the sky and tried to soak up its peacefulness. I wondered if, somewhere out there, God was looking back at me. I imagined Him in black robes, like a judge, deciding what to do with me. Lately, I'd done some pretty bad things. But if Polly was right, and God was really fair, maybe He'd understand that even though I'd made mistakes, I wanted to be a better person.

Although I was sorry I'd screamed at my mother, I wasn't sorry about what I'd said. I wanted her to change her mind about Polly. I wanted her to say, "All right. If she's your friend, I want to meet her. Ask her to come here." But there was one thing I did feel bad about—saying we were hardly Jewish. I guess I thought if I kept saying it, I might not get sent to hell.

Now I felt ashamed of myself for being such a coward. It must have taken so much courage for my grandparents to make their secret plan to send Mom and Aunt Bea away from the Nazis and their terrible war. So many millions had been killed! And Mom and Aunt Bea had had to be so brave to come to America by themselves. I felt like I'd let them all down. Saying I wasn't Jewish was like saying I wasn't a part of our family. But I was, and I wanted to be! Only I wasn't sure how to be Jewish.

The next morning when I came into the kitchen, Mom didn't look up from stirring her mug of coffee.

"I don't feel like eating now." I grabbed a banana from the fruit bowl. "I'll take this along with me for later."

Mom just nodded.

I pulled on my sweater, wondering if she was ever going to forgive me. I thought about apologizing, but I was afraid she might not accept. Besides, she'd been wrong, too.

"Lee?" Mom called when I was halfway out the door.

For a moment, my heart lifted. "Yes?"

"Come right home after school today."

• • •

Skipping breakfast meant I'd be too early for school, so I wandered around to the back of our building. I was thinking of trying something—if the alley was empty. I really didn't want to see Zeke.

It was empty, except for Lucky and the garbage cans. "Hi, cat," I said as I yanked off my sweater and sneakers. Then I took the green socks from my pocket and slipped them over my own white ones.

I looked around again to make sure no one was coming before I climbed on the railing that ran along the ramp to the basement. I teetered a bit while I fought to catch my balance. Then I closed my eyes and stretched out my arms. I didn't let myself think of anything except seagulls hovering.

"What are you doing?" a voice asked. Even before I opened my eyes, I knew it wasn't Peter Pan.

I sprang down from the railing. "I live here. What are *you* doing, Eddie?"

"I asked you first. Anyway, I bet I know what you were doing. You were trying to fly." Eddie was staring at my feet.

"I was not!" I peeled off the green socks and pulled on my sneakers. I was so angry, I could hardly tie the laces. "Do you know how much trouble you've caused?" I pulled the notes out of my sweater. "You put these in my desk. You took them from my secret place."

Eddie gave me one of his stone-faced looks. "So?"

"They were *private*. You read them!"

"So what? They're just bullcrud. People shouldn't go around judging each other as if they're God."

The way he said it, so fast and fierce, made me realize something. Eddie knew what it was like to be judged, too.

"Yeah, it's bullcrud," I muttered. I grabbed my books and started walking. Suddenly I remembered something. I pulled the banana from my pocket, peeled it, and broke it in half.

"Here," I said, handing him a piece. "We'd better hurry." But before I headed out of the alley, I lifted one of the trash-can lids and flipped the skin inside. I tossed in Mrs. Burke's notes, too.

I took tiny bites of banana, holding each one on my tongue for as long as I could before chewing. Eddie shoved his entire half into his mouth, which made his cheeks puff out like a chipmunk's. Gross! I could never really be friends with someone like him.

26

After school I played hide-and-seek with Mikey, which was hard to do in our tiny apartment. I was wedged behind the bedroom door when I heard the phone ring.

"Lee, it's for you," Mom called.

"Coming."

"Buh!" Mikey peeked behind the door, grinning his big, pleased smile. I gave him a tickle and went to get the phone.

From my mother's stiff expression, I could tell who it was. But I stretched out the cord and stepped into the coat closet, daring her to stop me. I was almost disappointed when I heard her go back into the kitchen.

"Hello?"

"Lee, the pirates are coming back tomorrow!" Polly said hurriedly. "Peter told me. You have to come over after school." It was easy for me to imagine her face. Her eyes would be enormous behind her glasses, and she'd have pink spots of excitement on her cheeks.

I closed my eyes. "I can't. I'm not allowed to."

"You're being punished?"

"Not exactly—I'm just not supposed to go to your house."

"Why? What did I do?"

"Nothing." I took a deep breath. "It's your mother. She gave me these notes that said I'd go to hell if I didn't convert."

"Oh, no." Polly sounded as if she'd already lost an argument—or a friend. "She does that sometimes. My mother believes it's her mission. She wants to save you."

"I don't need to be saved! I'm not bad, *I'm Jewish*."

"I know." Her voice sounded small and hurt.

"My mother found the notes. She had a fit," I explained. "I tried to tell her you didn't believe that stuff, but she doesn't care. Now I'm not supposed to see you anymore."

Neither of us said anything, but I knew Polly was still there. I held on and waited until I couldn't stand it anymore. "You remember how I told you that my Mom's parents died because their house was on fire and they didn't get out?" I asked. "You want to know who set that fire? Their Nazi neighbors! People who hated Jews!" I was whispering and crying at the same time, but I didn't care. "My grandparents stayed inside because they wanted to. They thought it was better to die at home than to go to the Nazi camps and die there."

"That's horrible!" Polly croaked. I could tell she was crying, too. "The people who did that were murderers. But my mother isn't like that!"

"My mom says the kinds of notes your mother wrote can turn people into beasts who do those things."

"Is that what you think of me—?"

"Of course not! I know you're not like that. You're the fairest person I've ever met. But my mom won't trust anyone who's not Jewish. That's why I can't come over. She's prejudiced, too."

"But I'm sorry about the notes," Polly said. "Can't you tell her?"

"It won't matter. She won't change her mind."

"Never?"

I felt like my heart was beating in my throat. I couldn't answer.

"*Lee?* Don't worry about the pirates tomorrow—I won't let them get away. Okay?"

I pressed the phone into my chest and waded deeper into the coats so my mother wouldn't hear me sobbing. When I could finally stop myself, I put the receiver to my ear again. "Polly?"

But a dial tone was my only answer.

27

Overnight, the sunny fall sky turned the gray-white color of smoke, and a cold, slapping wind came barreling through Brooklyn. "Looks like a storm's on the way," my mother said as she turned on the radio. "Maybe you should wear your raincoat."

But I wanted the safe, cared-for feeling of Aunt Bea's sweater wrapped around me. "My sweater's much warmer," I said as the weather report came on. "If it rains, I can put up the hood." I don't think Mom actually heard my answer. She was listening too hard to the weatherman.

Outside, the wind blew leaves and twigs at me. I clamped down my jaws and tasted grit between my teeth. Sometimes the gusts were so big, I had to lower my head to push through them. By the time I was passing the Burkes' house, rain was falling hard and fast. I turned my face to the sky so I could feel the cold needles on my eyes and cheeks.

"Boys and girls, there's a hurricane coming," Miss Hadley announced first thing. Her voice was calm, but her eyes had a shiny, excited look. "Observing a hurricane from a safe place can be thrilling. When I was a little older than you, I became very interested in studying storms."

She paused and let the class chatter for a few minutes. I looked out the window. A chain of charcoal clouds was headed toward us. Depending on how you looked at them—squinty-eyed or wide-eyed—they could have been a herd of wild beasts or a fleet of pirate ships. I wondered if Polly could see them from her classroom window.

On a table she'd dragged to the front of the room, Miss Hadley was setting up a strange-looking box on legs. It was made of wood, but it had three glass sides. There was a hole in the bottom and a metal stovepipe attached at the top. The lid also had a little box on one side with an electrical cord coming out. When Miss Hadley plugged it in, four lightbulbs in the top lit up the inside of the box.

"This was my eighth-grade science project," she told us, sliding an electric hot plate under the thing.

"It won third place in my grade. Does anyone want to guess what it is?"

We all sat there like cheesebrains. Even Mitchell. Miss Hadley's bright smile began to droop at the corners. "Doesn't anyone have an idea?"

Finally, Eddie raised his hand.

"Eddie?"

Wood creaked as the members of our class turned to stare.

"It could be a hurricane maker," he answered. "You heat up a pan of water, and it makes a cloud inside the box."

"That's right." Perfect Mitchell was looking at Eddie with his mouth open, but Miss Hadley didn't act the slightest bit amazed. "Would you help me show the class how it works?" she asked.

Eddie gave a tiny nod and walked stiffly to the front of the room. The look on his face dared anyone to make fun of him for being the teacher's helper.

While Eddie poured water into a pie pan and plugged the hot plate into an outlet, Miss Hadley explained that hurricanes in the northern hemisphere twist upward in a counterclockwise direction, and hurricanes in the southern hemisphere twist clockwise.

In a few minutes, the water in the pie pan began to boil. Then a steam cloud appeared inside our teacher's old science project. "We can make our storm change directions by sliding the glass panels left or right," Miss Hadley said. "Eddie, would you show the class?"

Eddie wiped his hands on his pants. He shifted the glass walls to the left, and the hurricane swirled counterclockwise.

"Oooh! Aaaah!" the class murmured admiringly.

"Now I'll move the walls to the right, and the hurricane will switch directions," Eddie said. He didn't actually look at us—he just kept his eyes on the box. In a little while, Miss Hadley's storm turned clockwise.

Suddenly there was a boom that made the floor shake and the windowpanes rattle. Outside, the trees bowed and shook. I lifted up from my seat and saw a huge, broken tree limb lying in the schoolyard.

"Wow, Eddie. You better not let that hurricane out of the box," Mitchell announced. "It'll bring the whole school down!" We all laughed, even Eddie.

While everyone watched out the windows, Eddie slipped back into his seat. I think I was the only one who was paying attention to him. At lunchtime, I noticed something else. He hadn't carved his desk all morning.

At three o'clock it was raining pretty heavily. The clouds were bunched together in a big dark mass. I could almost feel it pressing down on me.

"Everyone go straight home," Miss Hadley ordered as we filed out. "It looks like that hurricane's nearly on our doorstep." She gave us each a little pat on the shoulder as we passed her.

My sweater was soaked by the time I'd walked half a block. I wished I'd taken my mother's advice about the rain slicker. Water was dripping off the edge of the hood and onto my nose.

I felt the thunder rumbling in my chest before I actually heard anything. Then a crack, a crash, and a flash lit up the outlines of dozens of ships overhead, all creaking, rocking, and firing. It was as if the entire sky were at war. For an instant, I let myself look across the street at the big white house. Polly was leaning all the way out from the porch, staring up at the sky. I looked away before she saw me, and I started to run.

Another boom made me freeze just as a long black line came snapping down. It struck the sidewalk ahead of me, twitching and making sparks. I began edging toward it.

"Look out!" Someone grabbed me by the hood, and I stumbled backward into a bony chest. It was Eddie.

"Quit it!" I said, tugging away from him.

"That's a live wire. We have to go around it. Let's cross the street."

"No! I'll jump over." I was afraid to get any closer to Polly. Just the thought of it made my heart beat faster. I didn't know what to say to her. It was too hard and too sad.

"That line is dangerous, Lee! The wind could whip up anytime. You could be electrocuted." Eddie grabbed my arm and began leading me across the street.

The wind did pick up as we made it to the other side of Avenue J. I had to hold on to the green fence to keep from blowing away. I kept my head down, but I knew Polly was watching.

"Lee, hurry! Come up here. You can pull yourself along the railing," she called. There was no sign in her voice that I'd said I couldn't be friends with her anymore.

I wanted to so badly, it hurt. But it also hurt to disobey my mother. "You know I can't!" I yelled.

She pointed toward the sky. "Isn't it amazing? I told you they were bringing reinforcements."

I studied the fleet of cloud ships. It wasn't that I'd forgotten about Miss Hadley's hurricane experiment. I could explain how storms were created by heat and moisture out over the ocean. But why couldn't there be pirates hiding inside the hurricane? I was, after all, a person who had flown.

"This big one overhead must be Hook's!" Polly shouted.

I looked up at the dark hull of Hook's ship and shuddered. I told myself I wouldn't exactly be disobeying Mom if I just stayed on the porch to wait out the storm.

I looked at Eddie. His jacket was soaked, and he was shivering. But he was staring at me as if he didn't notice. "Come with me?" I asked.

He jerked his head as if to say okay. We dashed up the steps and out of the rain.

"Polly, this is Eddie," I said.

"Hi." She didn't act at all curious, but I was sure she remembered I'd once claimed I didn't know him.

The three of us stood under the shelter of the porch, watching the wind blow things along the street—leaves and sticks, newspapers, candy wrappers, a broken umbrella, and a black boot with a silver buckle that made me gasp. From several blocks away,

I could see two yellow spots bouncing up and down as they made their way toward us.

"Look, Eileen and Timmy!" I shouted when the spots got closer.

Polly ran down the block to meet them. She wasn't wearing a raincoat or carrying an umbrella. She was drenched and laughing when she came back, pulling the Kilkennys by their yellow slickers.

"This is Eddie," I told them. "We're in the same class."

Before either of them could act surprised, Polly said, "Well, come on, let's go inside. We have work to do."

"What work?" Eddie looked at me rather than at Polly.

But before I could answer, she said, "Pirate fighting. The attic's full of them."

28

The attic looked the same as always, yet something about it felt different. The air in the room was so heavy I could almost see it—a gray mist as if a cloud had drifted inside. Both half-moon windows were wide open. Rain was dripping off the sills and onto the bare floor.

When I listened closely, I could hear a low, thrumming sound. In my throat, I could feel my blood pounding to the same rhythm.

"Eileen, Smee's after you. I'll climb up the mast and drop the sail on him!" Polly shouted. She jumped onto the sofa and yanked something down. Eileen leaped onto a cushion and shoved as though her life depended on it. Screeching, she slid across the floor.

Polly pointed at a pile of sticks in a corner of the room. They looked like the ones we'd used to scare the blackbirds in the yard. "Timmy, quick! Get your sword! The crocodile's here!"

The word *crocodile* made my toes curl. Timmy grabbed a stick and began swinging it like a baseball bat. "Take that! Take that!" he piped in a high, excited voice.

"Lee, look out behind you!" Polly shrieked, just as I caught a whiff of stinking pirate's breath. I reached into my pocket, whirled around, and waved the Pirate's Booty at my invisible attacker. A haze of white dust floated in the air. Did I hear someone choke back a cough, or was it me?

"What's that stuff?" Polly called between cupped hands.

"Pirate's Booty. It turns pirates into gentlemen. Want some?" I waved the can and sprinkled a trail of powder across the floor.

"I need some! I need some!" Eileen wailed. She seemed to be wrestling with someone on her raft.

"Hold on, I'm coming." I skidded across the slippery floor and shook the can. A cloud of powder surrounded her like a magic mist.

"Oh, rats! I'm all tied up." Polly was lying on the sofa, writhing and twisting, but her arms appeared stuck at her sides. "Can someone cut these ropes?"

I'd almost forgotten about Eddie when he came bounding across the room. He pulled a pocketknife from his jacket and sawed through the ropes that bound Polly's arms.

"Thanks!" Polly leaped to her feet. "Oh, Lee—Captain Hook just flew through the window. He's up at the ceiling. Can you get him?"

I squinted overhead, trying to detect a shadow. I thought I might have seen something in the far right corner. As fast as I could, I pulled the magic socks out of my sweater and slipped them on.

The others got quiet while I climbed on the edge of the couch and stretched out my arms. I tried not to let myself think about them watching me as I closed my eyes and pictured the hovering seagull. I drew long, deep breaths until I felt myself growing light. And then I was lifting up. Flying!

I looked down at my band of gaping friends. Eileen had her hand over her mouth. The whites of Timmy's eyes were as huge as lightbulbs. Eddie's mouth was open in a perfect O. Even Polly had her hands clasped to her chest in amazement.

I shrieked as I felt something cold brush my face. It was sharp, like it might have been metal. I reached out to try to grab Hook.

"What's going on here?" a voice demanded.

"Mom!" Polly exclaimed.

In that instant I crashed to the floor.

I peered up at Mrs. Burke. Her face looked tight and angry as she gazed over the wet, powder-streaked floor, our scattered sticks, and our wild-haired, messy selves. Her narrow eyes landed on mine and stayed there.

I tried to stand, but when I leaned on my wrist, an awful pain shot up my arm. Tears leaked out of my eyes in spite of my efforts to stop them.

"I'm afraid crying won't help, Lee," Mrs. Burke said. "I invited you into my home. I tried to help you. But look at how you've repaid me—riling everyone up like this. I should have known better. You people always bring trouble."

29

Do you think you could go to school tomorrow?" Mom sat on my bed and examined my fingertips, which were sticking out from a cast that reached almost to my elbow.

"I still don't feel very well," I said, although my fingers were definitely less swollen and purple. "Besides, I won't be able to write."

"I'll bet you could learn to write left-handed if you tried."

When I shrugged instead of answering, my mother didn't act annoyed. She hadn't even gotten mad after I'd admitted falling in Polly's attic. I guess she thought a fractured wrist was punishment enough.

"Do you want to go for a walk with Mikey and me? Some fresh air might make you feel better."

"No, I'm too tired." I sank down into my pillow and pulled my soft blue quilt up to my chin.

"All right, then. We won't be gone long."

"Buh-bye," my brother said. He lifted a corner of the quilt to give my fingertips a kiss. I shut my eyes to keep a tear from sliding out.

It wasn't a lie about not feeling well. I felt sick every time I remembered how Mrs. Burke had called me "you people," as if I weren't a regular kid like the others. As if I were someone disgusting or dangerous. And I couldn't stop thinking about Polly. Three days had gone by, and she hadn't called. I wondered if she'd decided it would be better to find a new friend that her mother would approve of. Maybe she was right, but it made me feel bad—and mad, too.

I guess I fell asleep, because suddenly the doorbell woke me with a *buzzzz* that wouldn't stop. Someone seemed to have a finger stuck on the button.

"Mom?" I called. "Don't you hear the bell?" Then I remembered she'd taken Mikey for a walk. I wasn't supposed to answer the door when I was home alone. Whoever was there would have to go away and come back later. I closed my eyes and waited for the noise to stop.

But it didn't. I began to worry that it could be an emergency. Maybe Mrs. Feldman in 4D needed help. I trudged into the foyer.

"Who is it?"

"Eddie."

I stared at the old, brown door.

"I have your homework," he added when I didn't answer. "Miss Hadley made me bring it."

"Sorry. I can't let you in," I said, backing away from the door. "I'm not allowed."

"Cut the bullcrud and open up, Lee!"

"Shhh!" I was afraid Mrs. Feldman would call the police. With my left hand, I fumbled with the lock until I got it undone.

"Hi." Eddie stared at my cast.

"Hi." I held out my good arm for the books.

"They're pretty heavy. I'll bring them inside so your left one doesn't get broken, too." Before I could stop him, Eddie slipped by me and carried the stack to the kitchen table. It looked like Miss Hadley had given him everything in my desk and then some more.

"Gee, thanks."

"It wasn't my idea," Eddie answered, but he flashed his dogtoothed grin like he thought it was funny.

I flipped the pages of the book on top of the pile. "Look—don't tell anyone how I fractured my arm. Okay?"

"You mean falling? At least this time it wasn't off your bike."

"Not that—about what Polly's mother said."

Eddie shrugged. "Who cares what she said? It's bullcrud."

"I care!" I looked away quickly so he wouldn't see my eyes welling up.

"All right—I won't tell."

"Okay. Thanks." I thumped the stack of books. "I guess I'd better start my work now."

But instead of heading for the door, Eddie just stood there. Neither of us said anything. I was beginning to worry I'd have to push him out, when he cleared his throat. "I, um, wanted to say something about what happened in the attic."

I looked up.

"I saw."

"Saw what?"

"You know. I saw you fly."

"You did?" My stomach fluttered as if it was going to take off again.

"Yeah, a little." Eddie held his hands apart to show how high. It looked like about ten inches. "How'd you do it?"

I looked down at my feet in their fuzzy pink slippers. I could feel my face turning pink, too. What if he was making it up? If I told him the truth, he could use it against me. He could tell our entire class and make me look like a cheesebrain. I decided to take a chance.

"I have these socks that might be magic—" I began.

"They never made me fly."

I looked up at him so quickly, I felt dizzy. "What do you mean?"

"They're mine." Eddie's voice was suddenly hoarse. "My grandpa's old washing machine has been broken down for months. Zeke's been letting me use your laundry room. I met your mother down there, and she was nice. She offered to do my wash with your family's. I guess those socks got mixed up with your stuff." Eddie flashed me a funny half-smile. "I never got an inch off the ground in them."

30

After Eddie left, I went to the telephone. Right beside it was the number of the hospital. "I am a person who can fly," I told myself. Aunt Bea had been away for almost two weeks, and I hadn't talked to her at all. I'd been afraid she would sound weak and sick. I'd wanted her to be strong and well, in case I needed her.

"Hello?" My aunt answered right away. Her voice sounded whispery, but welcoming—as if she was happy to be getting a call.

"Aunt Bea? It's me, Lee."

"Hello, darling—is everything all right?"

"Fine," I said firmly. "Are you getting better? I miss you!"

"I am. But I miss you, too. And my kitchen! The food here is *dreck*."

I had to laugh because *dreck* means "dirt" or "poop." "I'm dying for your apple cake! When you come home, will you teach me to make it?"

"It will be my pleasure."

I rubbed my cheek against the phone. "When do you think that will be?"

"Soon, I hope. Your eleventh birthday's coming up—and I feel like going to a party. It's dull here!"

My birthday was November 2—a little more than three weeks away. I hadn't wanted to think about it. Without my aunt—or any friends—I hadn't felt much like partying. But if Aunt Bea came home, there'd be something to celebrate. "Okay. I'll blow up balloons and decorate the apartment. You can teach me the cha-cha-cha."

"I mean a real party." Aunt Bea's voice got a little stronger. "Let's go to the Mandarin Teapot—my treat. Invite your friends, too."

The offer made me swallow hard. "Okay."

When I didn't say anything else, Aunt Bea asked, "Is there something more you wanted to talk about?"

My throat filled up with love for her. "Yes. I wanted to ask if you could teach me about being Jewish?"

There was a little pause before she answered. "I

would like to do that very much. We'll start by lighting candles on Friday nights. I'll teach you the blessing. All right?"

"Yes." It was the only word I could get out.

"Good. It's settled, then. The nurse is here to take my blood pressure. Call me again soon, Sweetheart. Good-bye."

I wandered over to the windowsill to water my peanuts. They'd already split in half. Each one had a teeny plant growing out of its middle and the most delicate roots at the bottom. In another few days, the plants would be ready to put into soil.

Next to my peanuts, Mom had placed another pot of seedlings. They were tall and thin, and I could see buds forming between the leaves. I wondered what my mother was growing now.

I was identifying subjects and objects in my grammar workbook when Mom came in with Mikey. "Where did these come from?" she asked when she saw my tower of books.

"Eddie Wagner brought them over."

"That was nice of him." She went to the windowsill and examined the plants.

"What's in the pot next to my peanuts?" I asked.

"Flowers," she said, fingering a leaf. "Shasta daisies."

"Really? Those are the daisies Luther Burbank developed."

"I know," Mom said. "They're one of my favorite flowers."

For a moment, I imagined that the ghosts of Carver and Burbank were haunting our kitchen. But even I knew I was getting carried away.

"I spoke to Aunt Bea while you were out," I told Mom.

Her hand flew to her throat. "But I already talked with her today. How is she?"

"She says she feels like going to a party."

Mom raised an eyebrow. "Shouldn't she be taking it easy?"

"She wants me to have a birthday party at the Mandarin Teapot and invite my friends."

"All right. Who?"

I took a deep breath. "Polly Burke."

Mom gave me a long look. "We've already talked about this, Lee. I suggest you invite someone else."

"Polly's the only one I want."

"There must be someone in your class who—"

"It's *my* birthday, Mom." Suddenly I had to blink back tears. "Why can't you give her a chance?"

Without answering, Mom slipped an apron over her head. We were both quiet for a few moments. Then she said, "Even if you did invite Polly, I'm sure her mother wouldn't let her come."

While she started dinner, I set the table. I thought Mom was probably right about Mrs. Burke. But maybe if Polly worked on her, she'd say yes. People could change, couldn't they?

The next morning I piled my mountain of books into a shopping bag and hung the handle from my left arm. At first, I hurried as fast as I could with a lumpy bag of books and a cracked wrist. But when I realized the streets were empty and I was already late for school, I slowed down.

From across Avenue J, I studied the Burkes' house. The shades were pulled down, and it looked as if the place were asleep. Had the hedge grown higher around the porch? Had there always been a gull-shaped crack in the chimney?

I tipped my head back and studied the sky. The clouds were shapeless streaks of gray. There was no sign of a pirate ship, and I began to wonder if I'd ever really seen one. Maybe it was only the heavy sky and the bagful of books, but I felt so weighted to the ground, it was hard to believe I'd ever flown.

I bumped the shopping bag hard with my knee and turned the corner onto the last block. At the other end, my redbrick school sat solid and cozy in spite of the dreary day. Suddenly I couldn't wait to get there.

Uck-uck-uck-isss! Uck-uck-uck-isss!

I heard the bird before I noticed it. Big and black as a bad mood, it was sitting atop the yellow traffic-light opposite school. Below on the pole was the electrical box where I'd hidden Teena Weenie. It seemed like a long time since I'd thought about hiding anything there.

"I'm not afraid of you," I told the crow. Still, I didn't come any closer just in case.

The bird cocked its head and winked a shiny eye. I wondered if I was seeing things. Birds didn't wink, did they?

"This is silly," I said aloud, and crept a few steps closer. Then I noticed that the door to the electrical box was slightly ajar. I peeked inside. A bright green feather was stuck beneath a tangle of wires. Carefully, I plucked it out. Then I dug in my sweater pocket and pulled out the one Polly had given me—the one she'd called magic. They were exactly alike.

For a second my heart leaped with hope. I whirled

around, expecting to see Polly's face cracking up at how she'd fooled me. But there was no sign of her. I was so disappointed, I felt like going home to bed.

Uck-uck-uck-isss! Uck-uck-uck-isss!

I looked up at the crow. "You didn't put this feather in the box, did you?"

The bird hopped up and down on the traffic light. It seemed to be saying that I'd guessed right. I tried staring it in the eyes to see if it was telling the truth. But the silly thing kept twisting its neck back and forth as if it were trying to avoid my gaze.

"If you can understand me, say something!" I ordered.

Uck-uck-uck-isss! Uck-uck-uck-isss!

"Very funny!" Suddenly I felt like the world's biggest cheesebrain, talking to a bird. I picked up the shopping bag and crossed the street. When I got to the other side, I looked back at the traffic light. The crow was nowhere in sight.

Before I entered the schoolyard gates, I looked at the green feathers once more. Polly had told me that hers would grant one wish. Now perhaps I had two.

I brought my hand up to my mouth, palm flattened, and closed my eyes. I wasn't sure if early birthday wishes counted, but I made them anyway. "Go!" I whispered, and gave a long, hard blow. The feathers went floating in the air. For a moment, I watched them swoop and swirl among a rush of flying leaves. Then I hurried through the schoolyard gates.

31

A package of birthday invitations was waiting on the table when I got home. Each card had a bouquet of daisies on the front, with the message: *Birthdays are for sharing.*

"I thought you might have thought of some other kids to ask to the Mandarin Teapot," Mom said. "It's still not too late." Then she walked out of the kitchen, pushing the dust mop along the floor.

"I only want one person," I muttered, when I was sure she couldn't hear. But then a weird thing happened. The longer I sat there, the more people I thought of. I reached for a pen and started filling out invitations in my wobbly left-handed writing. The last one was for Polly.

I looked up the addresses in the telephone book. There was only one I couldn't find. After I'd stuck the stamps on the others, I called, "Mom, I'm going to put these in the mail." Before she could answer, I was out the door.

I ran all the way to the corner mailbox and practically threw the cards in the slot. I was having the most confusing feelings—as if there were two Lees in my body. "Mom is going to kill me," I told myself. And yet, at the same time, I felt calm and clearheaded. I knew what I had to do next, even though it scared me.

I found Zeke in the laundry room, fixing one of the washers. He was concentrating so hard, he didn't hear me come in—which was good because I didn't quite know how to start.

"Zeke? Do you need any help?" I asked.

He looked up and eyed me for a second. "I don't think so, thank you." He didn't even mention my cast. For some reason, that made me want to bawl.

"I could hand you the tools and put back the ones you don't need." I knew it wasn't much of an offer, but I didn't want to leave. I really needed to apologize.

To my surprise, Zeke said, "Do you think you can do it left-handed?"

"Yes." I leaned against the washer, next to his big red toolbox, and waited.

Zeke didn't talk at all while he worked, and I was

worried that if I did, he'd send me away. After a while, I thought he'd forgotten me—but then he held out a screwdriver. "Would you put this back and give me the wrench?"

I plucked it out and handed it to him. When he went back to tinkering, I tried straightening up his box, sorting nails and screws, grouping the tools, and putting them in size order. My fingers were a little clumsy, but I managed okay.

"Do you see the needle-nose pliers in there?"

I fished around in the box. "You mean these?" I held up a pair with thin silver pincers.

"Yes." He took them from my hand. This time he looked at me.

That gave me some courage—and a little hope. "Zeke? I want to apologize for what I said—about you being just a super. I didn't mean it."

He pushed back his cap and let out a sigh. "Well, I am the super of this building, Lee."

"But you're more important than that to me. You're my friend." On the last word, my voice cracked a little. "I'm sorry, Zeke. Will you forgive me?"

I hardly dared to breathe while he rubbed his chin and considered me. I thought about him, too—how he'd always been cheerful when he helped carry Deb up the stairs so she never had to feel bad about it, and how he'd tried to soothe me after she'd moved away by offering me a bike. I even thought about Eddie, and how Zeke had been teaching him to fix things. Zeke was as helpful and patient and understanding to us kids as Miss Hadley. He would have made a great teacher. I wondered if he'd ever wanted to be one, which made me realize something. We didn't have any Negro teachers in our school. Not a single one. I was beginning to understand what Miss Hadley had meant about things being unfair.

"All right, I accept your apology," he answered in a way that was slow and serious. He pulled down his cap brim and went back to working on the washer.

I knew there was a difference between forgiving someone and being their friend. I wondered if things would ever be the same again between Zeke and me.

I dug my hand in my pocket and felt the last envelope. "Zeke? I was wondering if you know where Eddie Wagner lives?"

"Mmm-hmm."

"I need his address so I can send him an invitation to my birthday party. I couldn't find it in the phone book."

"I do not know the exact address, but you could drop it off yourself. Ed lives two blocks away on East

Thirty-ninth Street. It is right around the corner from Avenue J—the third house on the right. He and his granddad have the basement apartment."

Zeke stood up. "This old washer is fixed for now. Thank you for your help."

32

The first thing I did when I came home each day was to check the mail. My heart would start racing as I flipped through the envelopes. A few times there was something from one of the kids I'd invited to my party. But there was nothing from Polly.

And even though I was disappointed—even though I'd flip through the envelopes again just in case—there was a little part of me that felt relieved. If Polly decided to come, I'd have to tell Mom I'd invited her. That thought made me feel like I was falling from a very high place.

Once, when I'd come back from doing an errand for Mom, I asked if there'd been any calls for me.

"Whom are you expecting a call from?" she asked.

I almost did it. I had Polly's name on my tongue.

But I froze up. "No one," I mumbled. After that, I didn't ask about phone calls anymore.

Although I'd been watching for mail every day, I was surprised one afternoon when Mom waved an envelope at me. "Letter for you," she said, and set it on the table. There was a big smile on her face as she left me alone to read it.

I grabbed it and ripped it open.

Dear Lee,

Thanks for the invitation. I really wish I could come, but on my allowance, I'd be at least ninety years old before I saved enough to fly from Briny Breezes to Brooklyn.

I'm glad you're not mad at me for not writing before. It was hard to make friends in my new school, at first. For a while, I didn't have anything good to say. And I guess reading about all your new friends (and your boyfriend!) made me a little jealous.

Then three good things happened: (1) My parents got me the cutest little terrier puppy—I named him Jay after "Avenue J." (2) I joined the chorus at school and have a solo for the Thanksgiving concert. (3) In chorus, I met Allison, and she is becoming a good friend.

But I still miss Brooklyn—especially you—a lot. I kind of miss Gary and Larry (don't you think they're sort of cute?). I even miss the Weenies, a little. (Ha! Ha!)

From now on, I promise to write more often. I hope you'll write back to me. Bon Anniversaire! (That's French for "happy birthday.")

Your friend forever,
Deb

On the night before my birthday, I couldn't sleep. Tomorrow was my party at the Mandarin Teapot, but I still hadn't heard a word from Polly. Suddenly, I was wondering if she'd received the invitation. What if it had been lost in the mail? Or if her mother had thrown it away?

Twice, when Mom was out, I tried calling Polly's number. The first time, no one picked up. But the second time, Mrs. Burke answered, and I hung up without saying a word. After that, I was afraid to call. And I couldn't help wondering why Polly didn't call me. Maybe she didn't care about being friends anymore.

Suddenly I had to find out. I had to ask her to come to the party in person. I wanted Polly to know that I didn't blame her for what her mother had said. I'd wanted to be in the attic just as much as she'd wanted me to.

But I'd waited too long—and now it was too late. There was no way I'd be seeing her before the party. Unless . . .

I got out of bed and went to the window. I'd never actually flown anywhere before, but I thought I could do it. Eddie said he'd seen me rise—almost ten inches. And I was sure I'd have gone higher if Mrs. Burke hadn't ruined things. I was already picturing Polly's amazed face when she saw me at her window.

I pushed up my own window as quietly as I could so Mikey wouldn't awaken. The cold, night air stung my cheeks and neck. I knew Mom would want me to wear my sweater—it was the least I could do. I figured I was already breaking enough rules.

But my sweater was in the closet near the front door. And Mom slept so lightly, she woke up if Mrs. Feldman coughed. I held my breath as I tiptoed to the closet.

Without turning on the light, I reached in and felt for my sweater. *Bang!* When I tugged at it, the hanger slipped and crashed onto the floor. I froze, waiting for Mom to spring out of bed and for Dad to be right behind her. But the two of them didn't stir at all. They must have been really tired.

Just in case, though, I crept back to my room on my hands and knees. I was already beginning to feel light-headed and floaty as I buttoned my sweater. "Good-bye, Mom and Dad. Good-bye, Mikey," I whispered. My brother's pudgy hand was sticking out of the crib bars, and I had an overwhelming urge to kiss it. But before I could cross the room, I felt a rushing sensation in my body, and I was lifted up and out of the window.

At first, looking down at Avenue J was more scary than exciting. All I could think of was crashing face-first onto the concrete sidewalk, or the cold steel roof of a parked car. But I relaxed when I realized that flying was like drifting on water. I even felt a gentle rocking that was like the swaying of the ocean out past the waves, though it was probably air currents causing that motion.

In a way, flying was easier than swimming. I didn't have to windmill my arms or doggie paddle. I just kept them stretched out and curved like a seagull's wings. Turning was simple. All I had to do was think about where I wanted to go, and my body headed that way.

The moonlight was the pale golden color of the champagne I'd had at Polly's. Against it, the shapes of trees, roofs, and chimneys looked as sharp as if they'd been drawn in ink. It gave our neighborhood a cleaner, neater appearance that made it seem like a fairy-tale town, not bustling, crowded Brooklyn.

I flew over the houses with the cracked driveways.

When I spotted the shape of a bike leaning against the side of one of them, I sank down low to the ground. I was able to see inside the basement apartment because there weren't any curtains on the windows. I looked in each one until I found Eddie asleep on his bed. It was pretty dark, but I thought I could see the invitation to my party on the table next to him.

He moved his arm across his face, and I suddenly felt embarrassed about spying. I was sure Eddie wouldn't want me to know he slept in his underwear. I rose up high again and darted away.

Instead of going straight to Polly's, I detoured to see Eileen and Timmy. I knew they lived six houses up the block from the Burkes'. The Kilkennys' house had a rusty red roof that made me think of their coppery hair. I flew around the second story and began peering in the windows.

I found Timmy first. He was sharing his bed with a scraggly stuffed monkey, which surprised me. Timmy always seemed like the kind of kid who might grow up to be a pirate. But with the monkey tucked beside him, he looked as sweet as Mikey, although I knew Timmy would have hated to hear me say so. I peeked at Eileen next. Her school uniform—plaid skirt and white blouse—was draped neatly over a chair. Tucked into a corner of the mirror on the wall was a snapshot of Eileen and Timmy with a woman I guessed was their mother. For the first time, I realized that the Kilkennys didn't have a father living with them. It explained why Eileen's mother was always at work and why Eileen was in charge of Tim. No wonder she seemed so nervous about him.

I turned and headed back toward the Burkes'. At first, I just circled the house, checking to see if anyone was stirring. But the lights were out and things seemed quiet.

Polly's room overlooked the backyard. Her shade was up, and moonlight was streaming through her window like a flashlight. She was lying on her back in her canopy bed, with the puffy quilt drawn up to her chin. I tapped three short times on the pane. Polly sat up so quickly it was as if she'd been waiting for someone. She looked around the room.

"Polly, over here!" I tapped again.

Her eyebrows perked up like a dog's ears. "Oh, my stars—Lee!" She ran to the window and pushed it open.

"I don't think I should come in," I told her. "I'm not even sure how long it's going to last." I looked down at the garden. It seemed awfully far away.

"But how—?"

"I don't know. It must have something to do with Peter and the pirates. And you—I had to talk to you. Otherwise I never would've tried this."

Polly pressed her palms together and held them to her chin. "I didn't think I'd see you again after what happened in the attic. I'm really sorry about what my mother said. After you left, we had a terrible argument. I told her she could never make me believe that God would send you to hell. But that if He did, I was sure He'd send me, too. I also said that you didn't rile up anyone—it was me. I was the wild one. I was the one she should blame."

"But I'm wild, too!" I burst out. "We're both wild, pirate-fighting girls." The thought made me grin. I reached through the window and touched her shoulder.

Suddenly, she noticed my cast. "Your arm! You broke it!"

I'd almost forgotten about the cast. It didn't even feel heavy anymore. "At least I got out of doing homework for a few days," I joked. "Besides, it's only a wrist fracture."

"The pirates are gone, you know. We got rid of them for good." Polly raised her eyes toward the attic. "Peter left, too. He said he had to help the Indians." Her smile seemed to come and go, as if she couldn't hold on to it.

I remembered how I'd felt when Deb had moved away, and I wasn't sure what to do next. I wondered if that was how Polly felt now. "Do you have a bike?"

"Yes."

"Do you want to go riding sometime?"

"Sure. When?" Polly looked down over the sill, as if she were ready to climb out.

"Next week—I'll let you know." But first, I promised myself, I was going to tell Mom about borrowing the bike. I thought it might be okay with her if I offered to do something to pay Zeke back. Maybe I could sweep the sidewalk in front of the house every day.

The corners of Polly's mouth began to curl. "I know this house that might be haunted. We could ride over there."

"Okay!" I was ready to take on a whole pack of ghosts. But I still had to swallow before I could get out the question I'd come to ask. "Are you coming to my party tomorrow?"

"I want to, but . . ." Polly looked back over her shoulder. "My mother won't let me."

I grabbed her wrist. "Maybe if you talk to her again—"

Suddenly there was a creak as the door to her room swung open.

"Polly? What are you doing up?" Mrs. Burke asked in a low voice.

"Nothing. I couldn't sleep."

"Why are you at the window? Go back to bed."

"I was just looking at the moon."

"Did you hear something out there? I thought I might have heard a voice." Mrs. Burke's slippers made slapping sounds as she crossed the floor.

"No, Mom." Before she turned away, Polly's eyes met mine. *"Quick, hide!"* she mouthed.

I let go of Polly and tried to dive beneath the window. Instead, I began falling. *"Go up!"* I whispered as my body kept on dropping. *"Up now!"* But whatever had been holding me up was gone.

33

The first thing I became aware of was the cold, hard surface underneath me. It didn't feel like grass, but it didn't feel like a mattress either.

Oh my God, I'm dead! I thought. Then my heart began to race, which made me realize I probably wasn't dead. I concentrated on opening my eyes, but my lids felt like there were quarters resting on them. Finally, I managed to force them up enough to peek. I was in my room, on the floor.

Slowly, I rolled my head toward the window. It was barely open enough for me to get through. How had I gotten back here? I looked down at my arm and saw the cast peeking out from the sleeve of my pajamas. But I wasn't wearing my red sweater.

In his crib, Mikey whimpered. My body felt limp as I pushed myself up off the floor and covered him with his blanket. Then I climbed into my own bed, squeezed my eyes shut, and tried to force back the tears. I didn't care if I hadn't really flown. But being with Polly had felt so real. She'd been my friend again. That was the part I wanted to be true.

"Happy birthday, Lee. Time to get up," Mom said.

Right away, I sat up and looked around. The window was shut tight. "Did you come in here last night?" I asked.

"No, why?"

"I was hot. I thought I'd opened the window."

"You must have dreamed it," Mom answered. "Funny, I found your red sweater on the floor in front of the closet this morning. I thought you might have been cold."

I was so confused I didn't say anything.

"Well, come on. Dad and I want to give you your birthday present, but you'll have to get dressed first." She pecked me on the cheek and headed out of my room.

Suddenly I couldn't wait another second before I told her what I'd done. "Mom, wait!"

I guess I sounded bad, because she whirled around and came back in.

"I have to tell you something. I . . . I invited Polly

to my party. I don't think she's coming, but—"

"Lee! How could you? You know I forbid you!"

I took a deep breath, and the words just came out. "I made a wish, Mom. But then I realized I couldn't just wait for it to come true. There was this little voice inside me saying if I believed in it, I had to make it happen. I don't know if that was God or my heart, but I figured either way I ought to follow it. Because it doesn't matter what Polly's mother says or does. All that's important is how Polly acts—what *she* believes. She knows her mother's notes are a bunch of . . . of . . . bullcrud." I took my mother's hand. This time, she didn't pull away.

"You never give up, do you?" She shook her head and sighed. "Well, maybe that's a good thing." She leaned over and kissed my forehead. "All right. If Polly comes, she comes. Now hurry and get dressed. Your present is downstairs."

Downstairs? I wondered if it was a little dog like Deb's. I jumped into my clothes and appeared in the kitchen without combing my hair or brushing my teeth. Mom smiled at me without seeming to notice. Dad lifted Mikey out of his high chair. Then our entire family hurried out the front door.

My present was a shiny red bike—*my borrowed bike*.

But now it had a little license plate on the back that said LEE.

"Zeke sold it to us for a very good price," Dad said. "And he got you the license plate himself."

"He did?" I ran my hand over the letters while I waited for the tears to pass. Maybe I could thank Zeke by sweeping the sidewalk or by making him an apple cake—as soon as Aunt Bea taught me how.

My father patted the bicycle seat. "Try it out."

I got on my bike and took off like a wild girl. I was eleven years old, and I could go anywhere I wanted—at least in Brooklyn. The only thing that would have been better was if someone was riding beside me.

We had two tables at the Mandarin Teapot for my birthday celebration. Mom and Dad were sitting at one with Aunt Bea and Uncle Harold. They'd had a booster seat set up there for Mikey, but my brother had climbed down and insisted on sitting with the big kids—Eileen, Timmy, Gary, Larry, Eddie, and me.

Besides the bike, my presents were a navy-blue sweater with pockets that buttoned, knitted by Aunt Bea; a copy of *Peter Pan* from Eileen and Timmy; and a softball and a mitt from Gary and Larry. Eddie's gift was the weirdest—a cactus with a flower growing out of the top.

"It reminded me of you," he said as he plopped it down beside my plate.

I eyed the spiky, pickle-shaped thing with its small red flower. It wasn't pretty like Shasta daisies. "Me? In what way?"

Eddie touched the tip of one of the cactus prickles and grinned.

I could feel a blush rising into my cheeks.

"Hey, you look like a glowworm now," Larry shouted. Gary began singing a silly song we all knew—*"Shine little glowworm, glimmer . . ."*

Then everyone laughed and I did, too.

I'd just sipped a mouthful of wonton soup when Eileen leaned over and whispered in my ear, "Lee, I dreamed you were in my room last night. It was so real!"

"You did?" I squeaked, and nearly choked. Eileen patted me on the back until I stopped coughing.

"You're weird, Lee," Timmy said.

For a moment, I closed my eyes and saw myself sailing over Avenue J. In the distance, I heard a strange tinkling noise. But then I realized it was coming from the chimes that hung above the Mandarin Teapot's entrance. I opened my eyes and blinked.

Polly was in the doorway with her dad right behind her. When Mr. Burke saw me, he gave a little wave, kissed Polly's cheek, and left her there. For a moment, she looked so pale and serious in her solemn, gray coat, I was afraid she'd changed somehow. But when I jumped up and ran to meet her, her face softened into the girl I knew.

"You came," I said into her coat collar as I gave her a hug. "I didn't know if you would."

Polly shot me a serious look. "I wouldn't miss my best friend's birthday party." Then her face broke into a smile.

"Definitely not," I agreed. I took her hand and led her to the table where Mom, Dad, Aunt Bea, and Uncle Harold were sitting. "I want you to meet someone," I told them. "This is Polly."